Hard Ass in Love

the
HARD, FAST, AND FOREVER
series

SASHA BURKE

Copyright © 2017 Sasha Burke

All rights reserved.

This is a work of fiction.
Any similarities to real people, businesses, events,
or places is entirely coincidental.
The author acknowledges the trademarked status of all
brand products referred to in this book without
the ™ or ® symbols due to formatting constraints.
Contents of this book may not be reproduced or
distributed in any format without the written permission of
the author, except in the case of brief excerpts used for
review or promotional purposes.

This book contains mature language and content,
intended for reading audiences 18+.

Previously published under the title *WORK ME UP*.
Story content remains unchanged. Copyright amended to
reflect new title in 2018.

Printed in the United States of America

Other Books by Sasha Burke

SEXY, FEEL-GOOD FUN
Hot and sweet HEAs with lots of schmexy good times

The HARD, FAST, AND FOREVER Series
BARE ASS IN LOVE *(Available Now)*
HARD ASS IN LOVE *(Available Now)*
GRUFF ASS IN LOVE *(Available June 2018)*

. . . . .

STEAMY & SWOONY ALPHAS
These heroes have <u>one</u> weakness they're finally giving in to…

The Off-Limits and HIS Collection
HIS SHY NERDGIRL *(Available Summer 2018)*

Nicole is without a doubt the oddest creature I've ever met.

As far as therapists go, she's pretty damn good, even though her methods are way the hell out there. And while she's been using my climbing gym for her afterschool sessions for years now, lately, I've been having a tough time getting her out of my head. But, there's a reason I've stayed unwaveringly single while raising my kid for the last decade, and the last thing I need is to have my world turned upside down by this sexy little smarty with her bleeding heart and her uncanny ability to push all my buttons. So, when the maddeningly persuasive woman manages to somehow goad me into an admittedly entertaining challenge, *obviously*, I know I should just walk away... But I don't.

Logan is without a doubt the most fascinating man I've ever met.

As far as billionaires go, he's hardly typical. He's practically allergic to the indoors, stubborn to the extreme, and an absolute teddy bear—of the burly, overprotective variety—when it comes to his daughter. I'm well aware that he thinks I'm a bit of a weirdo. And frankly, I'm good with that status quo, especially given our history. The last thing I need is to develop an ill-advised crush on the gorgeous workaholic with his quietly intense charm and his strange ability to make the air seem thinner. So, when the unfairly distracting man manages to Jedi-mind-trick me into letting him set the stakes for our fun little challenge, *obviously*, I know I should just walk away... But I don't.

*To my kids.
For reminding me each and every single day
why I love being a parent.*

I

| LOGAN |

I pull into the school drop-off loop and roll down my window while Hannah unbuckles in the backseat and climbs out of the car.

As is the case every morning, she doesn't just rush off; she comes up to my window to slap my outstretched hand in a lo-five—my cool dad out I give her in case her classmates are watching.

Ever since she started the fourth grade, I've wondered if this is the year it'd no longer be cool for her to give her old man a hug in public. None of her friends do anymore when their folks drop 'em off places, far as I've seen.

It's fucking tragic, if you ask me.

Aside from climbing, being a parent is the only other thing I felt *born* to do. Parenting solo all these years hasn't always been easy, but what great things in life are? I've loved every minute of raising my little girl—from the three a.m. feedings to the stuffed animal tea parties and everything in between.

So yeah, it's tragic to think that one day, the cool-dad lo-five will be all I get. And trust me, I've already got the whiskey bottle I'll be comforting myself with when it happens.

Today, thankfully, is not that day.

Hannah dives halfway into my driver's side window after the lo-five to give me a proper goodbye hug. "Love you, Dad. Have a great day at work."

"Love you too, Squirt. Go learn something important today."

I wait until Hannah's safely inside the fenced courtyard before starting the engine up again. It's then and only then that I finally acknowledge the supreme annoyance responsible for the incessant tapping on my window.

There's a reason I immediately roll my window back up after I get my daughter's hug. Learned my lesson after one of the other kid's moms mistook the front of the school for a single dad pick-up site and practically suffocated me with her triple-d's leaning in to make inane small talk while ignoring my polite requests for her to leave me the hell alone.

Kid you not, I was all but ready to pop one of her implants by rolling up my window on the inappropriate woman's overinflated chest. But, I took the high road and simply turned on my windshield wipers so she got doused with blue window washing fluid instead.

Normally, I'm not a dick to anyone, let alone a woman, but I've got a short fuse for crap, and in situations like that, I reserve the right to earn the title of *king* dick.

Unfortunately, that moment of infamy seems to have turned me into some sort of damn unattainable unicorn or something for the other single (and some *not* single) moms, aunts, and even some cougar grandmas in the market to hook up with me despite my king dick crown…for reasons I can only attribute to my sizable net worth.

At least for the most part. Some of 'em have told me they're more interested in the size of my *other* reputed assets. Either way, now, every other week or so, another scantily-dressed woman with a face full of make-up will make her way over to my car.

It's fucked up.

I rev my engine, but the woman with the sprayed-on dress next to my car won't budge.

"What?!" I demand finally, opening my window a crack and no more.

She immediately pulls a piece of paper from her overexposed cleavage and slips it through the window gap.

Okay, first things first. I don't know about other guys, but me, I've never found the whole I-store-random-shit-between-my-tits thing at all sexy. You don't see men winning women over by reaching into the crotch of their pants to pull out things they've been keeping between their balls.

And secondly, a woman who hands me a graphically pornographic proposition along with her number in an elementary school parking lot definitely deserves a response from me. So, I grab a pen and scribble a reply. Then I flick the paper onto the gravel behind her, forcing her to back off enough that I finally have room to get out of there.

I take off before she can get all butt-hurt over me writing down what I did.

To be fair, she was the one who brought up the TMI status of her wet panties. I—helpful guy that I am—simply informed her there were discreet new incontinence pads and remarkable new medications to help her with her bladder control problems.

Good riddance.

I swear, I'm normally a perfectly nice person. In fact, that's kind of my reputation. "One of the nicest billionaires you'll ever meet," a reporter once called me. And when it comes to the women I go out with on occasion, I'm usually charm personified.

So yeah, it takes kind of a lot to aggravate me to the point of—

Fuuuck.

What timing. My thoughts about women who get under my skin are cut-off by the sight of a very noticeable teal SUV parked next to my reserved spot outside my climbing gym.

Nicole's getting an early start this morning.

Great.

"We're still closed," I say as I walk up to the employee entrance where she's waiting for me. "You know this."

"Would you consider letting me in a teeny bit early today? Just this once?" she asks, her playfully coaxing smile transforming her face to something almost mythologically tempting.

Yeah...this is why I don't let the woman smile this close to me.

Seriously, why is she here so early this morning? This is the first day in *months* that I don't have a packed AM schedule filled with back-to-back meetings and phone conferences. I was going to use the unprecedented down time to do some climbing.

I haven't even had a chance to climb in the new twenty-story wing I just added here in the expansion remodel—a thing of beauty, really. Measuring in as some of the tallest indoor climbs in North America, half of it consists of architecturally complex walls for sport climbers looking for extreme structural challenges. The other half is for outdoor climbers, fully constructed out of organic materials to simulate natural, craggy terrain and designed as topographical replicas of my favorite mountain faces and caverns, complete with panoramic glass windows for the former and encased cave-like features for the latter.

I fucking need to get on one of those walls today.

"Come back after we open," I say tersely, picking up my pace a bit to beat her to the door. Not really a big feat seeing as the woman is a good foot shorter than me, with cute, shapely legs that require two strides for every one of mine.

She keeps up with me. Persistent little thing.

And now I can't stop looking at said legs. Between those gorgeous stems and the rhythmic bounce of her full breasts thanks to the near jog she's in now, this is officially the most I've given thought to the woman's highly distracting body parts in all the time I've known her.

"If the positions were reversed," she says plaintively. "I'd be more than happy to open up for you and let you in."

Dammit, she'd be easier to deal with if she were saying that as a dirty come-on. She's not. She just says these weirdly seductive things by accident all the time…something I'm trying to explain to my dumb cock as I punch in my security code and pull out my key to unlock the door.

But Nicole beats me to the unlocking part.

What in the world?

"Why do you have Derick's keys?" My gym manager's novelty 'BREAK IN CASE OF EMERGENCY' plastic condom keyring is hard to miss.

There's an odd haze tunneling my vision on those set of keys in her hand. If I start letting my imagination conjure up reasons why she has another man's keys at this time of day, there's a good chance I'll do something supremely stupid.

Like haul her back to my car so I can make her come so hard she'll never even *think* about having something that belongs to another man in my presence again...

"I called Derick up and asked if he could let me in early," she says. "He's inside eating breakfast. I just came back out to grab my MP3 player from the car."

If she already had a way to get in, why on earth did she insist on me letting her in?

There's probably a psychological reason for it—there always is with her. I should just drop it before she starts with the shrinky stuff. But first, I have to fucking know...

"Why'd you call *Derick* instead of me?" I growl.

"Because I knew you'd be dropping Hannah off at school."

She's always so maddeningly logical. "How did you even get his number?"

"He gave it to me," she says slowly, like she's talking to a person who may have possibly sustained a blow to the head.

Maybe I have. Derick giving out his number to women who come in here isn't exactly an uncommon occurrence. As long as he works hard, which he does, I could care less who the horndog hits on.

Unless it's Nicole.

She bumps the door open with her hip. "You okay? You look like you're in a bad mood." She tilts her head sympathetically. "Let me guess, you got hit on at Hannah's school again?"

I scowl. "Yes."

"Oh, you poor, poor hot man with all the rabid women throwing themselves at you."

I know that's more of a dig than a compliment, but hell, I like her saying that I'm hot.

She steps past me through the door and her sweet floral scent sucker punches me in the face, about a split second before her soft, expressively attentive gaze delivers a blow to my solar plexus.

Okay, I lied before. I've allowed myself to think about *one* body part on Nicole Shaw quite a lot over the last couple years. Those smart, watchful eyes of hers. A shade of green you only see in nature. Always clear and candid. Never jaded or uncaring.

For crying out loud, does she have to be so goddamn pretty?

And not just a normal pretty, either, but a cute, refreshing kind of pretty that I always steer clear of when I make my one night stand selections. Too easy to like, too dangerous to get involved with. It's not really a rule, but I should probably make it into one.

SASHA BURKE

You'd think her being such an odd duck would offset even her specific brand of pretty. It doesn't. It somehow adds to it, makes her sexier. To me, anyway.

"So," she says quietly, breaking into my thoughts. "How's Hannah doing?"

Really, I should be used to her catching me off guard by now. Half the time, I never know what she's going to say—whether she's going to go brainy data queen or kooky hippie zen on me.

This time though, it's not what she's saying, but *how* she's saying it that's throwing me for a loop.

She's using her therapist voice on me.

Shit.

2

| LOGAN |

Any other day, I'd think her question perfectly harmless. But, I know for a fact that yesterday, half my staff blabbed to Nicole about some stuff Hannah's been having to deal with at school lately.

"Hannah's fine," I say curtly. "It's just a rough patch."

"I'd really like to make sure she's getting through it okay."

Man, that hypnotic voice of hers is something else.

"You grilling him on Hannah?" Derick asks her while munching on some breakfast burritos behind the cashier counter.

"Not grilling. Just talking," she replies diplomatically.

Derick shakes his head. "Don't hold back. Bust his balls. You're the expert on this stuff."

When she turns her attention back to me, armed with that validation, his eyes promptly drop down to her ass, openly admiring it like usual.

I want to fucking hit him.

Her big green eyes grow soft with concern. "You should let me work with her. Not in an official capacity of course since she isn't a student at one of my schools. But if she and I could maybe sit down for a bit and —"

"There's no need for that; she's fine," I say sharply, nipping that idea in the bud. "All kids go through crap in school. If you make a big deal out of it, it'll just upset her more."

I stop for a sec to shake hands with a longtime vendor who wants to leave new samples for me to check out. The handshake turns into an impromptu investment pitch on his part, per usual, and then 'a quick question' from a nearby staff member turns into a ten-minute meeting that really should've been scheduled with my personal secretary first.

And just like that, the white checkered flag for my day is dropped and the next hour zips by with one thing after another.

So much for getting in a climb this morning.

When my phone finally stops ringing, I get up to peer out the wide picture window behind my desk, overlooking some of the steepest climbs in my gym—walls I used to be up on at least a couple times a week when the gym first opened.

Jesus, I miss being out there.

To be honest, even I didn't anticipate these climbing

gyms to do this well in the U.S., let alone be launching internationally as well. It's a good problem to have, I know, considering I hadn't built this first gym with an entire future franchise in mind.

Energy utility development and ecotech marine research are where I made my billions. Climbing was just my hobby investment that just happened to become colossally successful.

In the beginning, it was a win-win. Getting to climb in gyms of my own design with walls and gear of my precise—admittedly very selective—choosing was my one escape that I used to be able to squeeze in during my work weeks, no matter how busy I got. And opening locations in all the main cities I traveled to most often was again, partly to that end.

But now, ironically, they're all doing so well, I'm too busy to be able to make use of them.

A soft knock at my door pulls me away from the window and back to my responsibilities. When I turn, however, I'm surprised to find Nicole in the doorway.

Puzzled, I motion for her to sit. "Everything okay? You haven't been waiting for me all this time, have you?"

"Logan, your daughter got *bullied* at school," she bursts out, continuing our earlier conversation right where we left off. "So, I *am* going to make a big deal out of it. Because it *is* a big deal."

Holy shit, the woman knows how to push my buttons.

"You think I don't know that?" I snap. "You think I haven't been thinking about this nonstop? You think I don't want to go out and find the little punks and kick all their dads' asses?"

She pauses and then smiles encouragingly. "That's good."

Just when I think she can't get any more perplexing. "Rage-filled violence is good?"

"Not the violence part, but the rest of it, yes. The last part says a lot about your own positive self-image," she answers in her token brainy fashion, which, combined with her throaty, lilting counseling voice, is starting to sound a little 1-900 to me.

I really shouldn't engage in all this psychological mumbo jumbo with her. Not with the way it's bizarrely starting to turn me on. But, I'm curious about her last assertion. "Explain."

"Fathers who value taking responsibility for their own children usually have the same high expectation of other fathers. Ergo, you're a good dad. I know that I for one most certainly think you are based on all the conclusive evidence I've seen of your parenting over the years."

I think that's the first time she's given me a compliment of that magnitude. The fact that the simple statement is making me feel ten-friggin-feet tall is a little disconcerting.

"Do you not want her to get counseled at all, or just

not by me?" she presses on.

I may as well be honest, since she asked and all. "Your therapy methods are a little..." I tread lightly, not wanting to insult her. Even odd birds deserve a gentle touch. "Unorthodox."

"This is true," she agrees. "But they're also highly effective."

Okay, I'll give her that.

"Do you want to walk around and argue?" she asks. "It'll make for a more focused argument."

Seriously, she's so strange.

Stranger still is the fact that I'm getting up and following her.

We fall into step in silence and I try not to notice that I can practically see down her damn shirt. Hell. I've seen perfect breasts before. Why are hers screwing with my head this much?

"You've witnessed firsthand how many kids I've helped through my counseling techniques," she reasons as we pass through the sitting area with the panoramic view of the north wing of the gym, both of us waving hi to the regulars. "What exactly are your concerns?"

"You work mostly with teens and college kids. Hannah's only nine."

"So, you think I'm not qualified to help her?"

That'd be a lie and we both know it. Nicole is nothing if not impressively qualified as a therapist. She's gotten to be a good climber, too. Ever since she's started using my gym regularly for some of her therapy sessions, I've been getting to see her in action a lot. And from what I can tell, she gets results.

Which is all well and good...for someone *else's* kid. Not mine.

"Look, I just don't want Hannah climbing, okay?" There, I said it. The CEO of one of the fastest-growing indoor climbing franchises in the U.S. doesn't want his daughter climbing. So, sue me. Even with all the proper harness gear, injuries can still happen, especially for younger, inexperienced climbers.

"I don't care how many precautions you take, or how safe my walls are, I don't want her up there. And I for *damn* sure don't want her going out on one of your outdoor climbs."

"I know," she replies softly.

Way to take the boom out of my bomb. "Then why are you hassling me about all this?"

"Because I also know you're quite possibly the most loving and doting father I've ever encountered. You'd do anything for that little girl. You know full well that climbing is only one of my methods, and yet you don't want me to work with her at all. So, I repeat, what exactly are your concerns?"

"I thought you had an early client this morning," I say, changing the subject.

"Nope. I actually don't have an appointment for another hour and a half. I just wanted to come in before you got too busy so we could chat about Hannah."

I frown. "You could've just called. You've got my number."

"I wanted to be sure you wouldn't hang up on me when I started pushing too hard."

Yeah, that does sound like something I would do.

"Is it…" she begins, but then stops, a little blush creeping over her cheeks.

Hell, I really want to know what was supposed to come at the end of that. "Is it…what?"

She straightens her shoulders. "Is it because you overheard my conversation with my students who were commenting on your...err...looks the other day?" she asks looking about as comfortable as a cat in a bath.

When I grin in remembrance of the day in question, she lifts her chin and injects a little more steel in her spine as she says simply, "Because the girls asked me outright if I thought you were handsome. And it would've been unethical of me to lie to them. I'm someone they trust, and that trust means I can't—"

"So, just to recap," I interrupt, unable to resist teasing her. "You think I'm both hot *and* handsome?"

Her blush deepens. "We're getting terribly off track here." She turns away from me to peer over the railed balcony, down at the climbers gearing up below. "I only brought that up to ask if my comment is perhaps making you feel uncomfortable with me," she explains.

Uncomfortable? No. Unbelievably tempted? Hell yes.

I come up behind her—close, but not quite touching—amazed to find that even as little as she is, her body still lines up with mine pretty goddamn perfectly.

This is information I *really* don't need to know.

Before I can make any further mind-messing discoveries about Nicole's body, however, a terrified shout from somewhere in the gym has us both shoving away from the railing and racing down to the main floor.

3

| LOGAN |

A full minute passes and we still can't pinpoint where the sound of distress came from.

I've got a couple dozen workers stationed around the 50,000 square-foot space, but per protocol, they each stay to monitor the climbers in their zones. So far, none of them can offer me any insight as to which section to head to. And with every passing second, I feel the atmosphere in the gym changing. The rumbling murmurs are growing louder, and climbers on every wall are starting to stop mid-climb to find out what's going on.

Shit, we need this contained *now*. The last thing we want is panic to set in and begin spreading like wildfire.

It takes another minute of searching, but finally, I spot him.

About four stories up on one of the inverted overhangs. His death grip on the wall is way too tight, and his entire frame is completely seized up in terror.

He's one of Nicole's college kids; I'd recognize the big bruiser anywhere.

Why the hell is he up there on his own? A couple of her students have been known to freeze up from time to time on the higher climbs, but usually, she's here with those climbers to get them through it.

"Oh my god, that's Kenny," she confirms. "He isn't supposed to go on the advanced walls without me."

Up top, I see one of my workers, Becca, coming down and across from the east to get to the frightened kid. But, when her rappel rope swings over to him, Kenny jerks to avoid it and slams his head into the wall.

Instantly, he loses his bearings. His anchor foot slips off the foothold a moment later, leaving him frantically searching in vain for something else to secure his foot to.

I whistle up at Becca and she immediately halts, holding her position on my command to keep from rattling him even more.

"Kenny," calls up Nicole then in the now silent gym. "I'm right here. Just focus on my voice. You need to regain control of your situation. Just like always. I know it's hard, but you can do this. I know you can."

Her voice is almost shockingly soothing. I've been through this dozens of times and I've never once been able to fake it that well.

Kenny manages to get his foot back in place, but even from down here, I can tell that's not going to be enough.

The way he's holding himself, he's clearly starting to have the shakes.

It's not muscular, it's mental. His body's shutting down from the fear, and if he can't rein it in, he'll fall. What worries me the most is how he's tangled himself up in his ropes with his thrashing. Coming off the wall with his lines wrapped around him like that, his injuries could be substantial.

"Nicole! I can't do this! You have to help me!"

Damn it all to hell. Before I can stop her, Nicole shoots forward and starts charging up the wall like a fucking superhero spider.

She's incredible. And she's making me scared shitless the higher she goes.

No one, I mean no one is allowed to go up without gear in my gyms.

She stops just below the forty-foot mark, near enough to talk to him, but far enough away that he won't take her down off the wall with him if he falls.

She's good. Really good. None of us would've been able to calm the kid down any faster, any better. The shakes seem to be gone now, and she's getting him to carefully detangle his lines.

That said, the one feeling the most fear at the moment is probably me.

Nicole's steady as a rock. Fierce, focused. But she's been hanging up there in one spot on a fairly graduated incline route for almost five minutes now, and that's *after* racing up faster than she should've. I know she's got to be aching by now. Climbing without gear is all around more intense. Much more exhausting. The added mental and emotional exertion means increased muscular strain and fatigue, which can push even strong climbers to their limits.

When the kid slowly, awkwardly starts to rappel down the wall, I signal Becca to shadow him. Then I return my focus to Nicole. She hasn't budged. All her attention is on Kenny as he makes his way down. I want to shout at her to stop being a goddamn hero and get moving. But I know she won't.

I start seriously fucking praying to whoever is listening when she finally begins her descent, silently whispering for her to keep her hold, to stay in her safe space mentally. Every bit of her needs to focus on this.

She's at the thirty-foot mark still on an inverted plane when I see her fingers slipping from the handhold. I react, rushing to get under her to at least break her fall.

Barely, just barely, I manage to catch her by the waist before she hits the floor. It's likely I bruised half her ribs in the process, but at least her legs aren't broken.

I yank her in close, locking her tiny frame against me so tight I can feel her pounding heartbeat against my chest.

Nothing else is even registering right now. She's safe; that's all my brain can process.

We stay there like that for a while, long after my lungs

remember to keep breathing and the absolute horror I'd felt starts dissipating.

Maybe it's the adrenaline. Maybe it's the fact that I finally have her soft curves in my arms. But I don't want to just keep holding her. I want to kiss the absolute hell out of her.

I don't though.

And the reason why is the very thing she was trying to get me to confess earlier.

It's why I've always kept my distance.

"Thank you, Logan," she whispers softly before gently disengaging from my iron grip.

She hops down and smiles at the gathered crowd. "And that's why we never climb without gear, ladies and gentlemen!" she calls out, trying to lighten the mood.

A quiet group chuckle ripples across the onlookers, more nervous than humorous, but thankfully, the heavy fog of apprehension starts to lift, and people begin climbing again.

I watch as Nicole flexes her cramped fingers and surveys her now broken, bleeding nails—just like I'm doing—before she sticks her hands in her pocket and beelines straight for Kenny to check on him.

"Man, she's amazing," I hear Derick say from behind me and I glare at him. The way he's staring at Nicole is making my blood boil. I know I don't have a claim on her, but still.

SASHA BURKE

I wait until she's done talking to her student before snagging her gaze. Then I jerk my chin over to my office. My silent demand is practically Neanderthal, I know.

Thank hell, she follows.

4

| NICOLE |

His confidence in me is shaken; I'm sure of it. Frankly, I don't blame him. This is the absolute worst thing he could've witnessed.

Kenny is a troubled guy with a lot of hardships in his life and a variety of mental health issues that have plagued him through high school. Unlike most of my other students, he also sees a psychologist for traditional behavioral treatments and a psychiatrist for medication. But now with the difficulties he's been having being in college with no foster family anymore, he's needed to adjust his meds quite a bit, which hasn't been an easy transition.

Not that I can legally divulge any of this, of course.

"What the hell *was* that out there?!" Logan bellows the second his office door slams shut, anger throbbing in his voice, his chiseled jaw locked with tension.

"An unfortunate, but highly atypical situation, Logan. As you well know, none of my students have ever been in danger like that before. People freeze up on the wall for a lot of different reasons, it's part of the therapy process. If Kenny hadn't been climbing without me to begin with, things never would've gotten to that point."

He looks exasperated as he stands there towering over me at his full height just north of six feet. Like an impossibly tough, complex, *daunting* mountain a climber would have to be a little crazy for wanting to take on. As a therapist, I don't really like using that word, but good lord, I might be feeling a little crazy right now.

"I'm not talking about the kid," he growls, "I'm talking about *you.* You went up almost four stories without gear. What the fuck, Nicole."

"If I hadn't, Kenny would've gotten seriously injured." Given how on edge Logan is at the moment, I know I should probably leave it at that, but I keep going. "I would do it all over again if I needed to."

"Jesus Christ. Are you *trying* to get me to take away your climbing privileges?"

I gasp. And then narrow my eyes at him. I don't like being threatened. "You would make me move all my students to a different gym?!" Not that any other gym is even on my radar. Logan's is bar none the best.

He glares right back at me. "I mean climbing privileges *anywhere.* I'll make sure you're blacklisted from every goddamn gym on the west coast."

He wouldn't!

Expression harsh and unyielding, he crosses his arms over his chest and reads my mind. "Oh, I would, sweetheart. You can't be reckless on a climb. I won't allow it."

"That was a calculated risk. And a *necessary* one," I argue. "You know me. I don't have a reckless bone in my body. I'll sign a waiver if that's what you're worried about."

"I don't care about that shit," he snarls. "I care about *you* not cracking your head open. Or worse." Raw, sincere, and outright *pissed-off* concern is slashed across his expression.

Not going to lie, hearing that Logan Reynolds cares about me in any context is a little surreal. And strangely intoxicating.

But, instead of overanalyzing the situation like I would normally, I frame the situation in a way that I know deep down he doesn't want to think about.

"What if that had been Hannah up there?" I ask. "Would you have objected to me going up without gear to help her? Would you have stayed down here yourself?"

His hands curl into frustrated, white-knuckled fists. He doesn't answer.

I venture a step closer, resisting the urge to calm him with tactile contact. Somehow, I don't think placing my hand on any part of his hard, musclebound frame right now would do either of us any good.

"Logan, if you can honestly tell me that what I did

was *wrong*, not just dangerous or scary, but actually *wrong*, then I swear to you right now I'll never do anything like that again."

He hisses his displeasure at my words, shoving his hands in his pocket and grudgingly maintaining his silence.

I breathe a sigh of relief. "If you let me work with Hannah, I assure you that I'll take the same kind of calculated risks to ensure her safety."

His gaze is equal parts annoyed and incredulous when he finally says, "You don't argue fucking fairly at all."

I smile. That's the nicest thing he's ever said to me.

Gazing at me with hooded eyes, he asks quietly, "You *really* think Hannah needs therapy?"

"It wouldn't be therapy. Any time I put in with her will be totally pro-bono."

He gives me a dry look. "Is that your nice way of telling me I can't afford you?"

Ah, humor. Now we're getting somewhere. "If I charge you, she'll become one of my therapy clients, which I honestly don't think is necessary at this point. I just want to teach her some overarching techniques that could help her out. That's all. It'll just be me hanging out with my friend's daughter."

Maybe I'm reaching by calling us friends. I've known the man for years, but he hasn't exactly been 'friendly' with me during all that time. Respectful, yes. Cordial, sure. But fairly distant, always.

"Anyway," I continue. "We can add in the climbing part later, only if you're both comfortable. In her case, I think she would really benefit from it."

He grunts. It's a thoughtful grunt, but I can tell he's still not fully on board.

"Do you promise to be doubly careful with her up on the wall than you are usually?" he asks then. "Not just because she's younger, but because she's my kid?"

I can't help but smile over that. Most folks would've worded that in reverse. The man is like a big, growly grizzly bear, fiercely gentle with no one except his cub. "I promise," I say

I arch an eyebrow at him then and toss back, "Do *you* promise to not be overbearing and overprotective and over-questioning of my methods at every turn?"

"*Hell* no."

It was worth a shot. I grin up at him. "So, are we doing this?

"I'm still not convinced she needs this."

"Duly noted."

"This better not interfere with her schoolwork."

"It won't."

"You better not change her. She's perfect the way she is."

Gah, this man. "I think she's pretty special, too, Logan."

He mulls this all over for another few seconds, pacing

and running a conflicted hand through his thick, chestnut brown hair, mussing with it at every pivot.

It's almost unfair that the more he musses, the sexier he gets.

Eventually, he stops and gives me a look. "My agreeing to this doesn't mean I don't still think you're more than a little nuts half the time."

"I'm totally okay with that. A little proud, to be honest."

His lips twitch up at the corner. "Okay then. You have my permission to talk to her about this or whatever she needs to work through, so long as you don't go all full-therapist on her. And from there, if she says she wants to climb, I'll let her go up with you once a week to start."

Victory!

"And…thanks. For wanting to help," he adds gruffly.

Aw. Bigger victory. But this one has me more melting than pumping my fist in the air. "Entirely my pleasure, Logan."

Dammit, why did that come out so breathy and…suggestive? "She's a great kid," I add quickly. "I've always thought so."

A pride-filled, affection-lit grin softens his expression at my compliment. As far as I'm concerned, these adoring, overprotective papa bear tendencies are just the most heartbreakingly attractive qualities in the male species.

"Thank you for catching me when I fell earlier," I say

then for reasons I can only attribute to an impaired mental state affected by my floating around in a puddle of swoon.

His eyes darken at the reminder of my fall.

Shoot! Just when I'd managed to defuse things. I brace myself for more shouting.

But his voice is quiet this time. "If you'd gotten hurt out there…"

His eyes search my face like I've got answers to questions he can't ask. "That would've fucked me up big time. I probably would've needed therapy or some of your psychological voodoo. Which means I would've made damn sure to ride your ass during your rehab until you got well enough to get back to work and be my therapist so you could shrink my head back to normal. So…yeah, it's a good thing you didn't get injured."

Goodness gracious, the man just has no idea how sweet he can be sometimes.

5

| NICOLE |

My stupid, confused heart is going haywire over his words, slamming against my ribs and making me lightheaded.

It doesn't help one bit when I see his gaze drop down to fixate on my lips. It makes me powerless to stop the urge to fixate on his lips as well. Or the thousand other perfectly beautiful things about the man.

All this time, I've been so careful about overlooking how attractive he is. I've sort of been thinking of him like a breathtaking masterpiece you see in a museum. The kind you're only allowed to look at from behind the velvet rope and *never* touch. If you *do* try and touch it, alarms will blaze and armed guards will tackle you to the ground.

Yep, that's been Logan for me.

But now, here he is, letting me behind the velvet rope, giving me a private showing, even.

I have to be honest, without the threat of alarms and

armed guards, I'm really worried I'm going to reach out and touch the no-touching masterpiece. Who hasn't wanted to run their hands over a sculpture before? Or feel the rough canvas of a stunning work of art?

Seeing him this closely for the first time in all the years we've known each other, I realize that his classic good looks are far less All-American country boy than I once thought... *especially* when he's looking at me the way he is now.

Those intense, piercing amber eyes of his have always been a weakness of mine. Especially when they darken to that warm, woodsy tone it does when he smiles (there's a reason I don't look directly at him when he's in a good mood).

Okay, museum's closed. Now just avert your eyes, Nicole. Or shut them. For chrissakes, just stop looking at the ridiculously gorgeous man.

I choose to ignore my brain's perfectly wise instructions for a change. In fact, my ability to be rational seems to be short-circuiting altogether. All thanks to the proximity of Logan's tall, ripped body—perhaps the most magnificently muscled build I've ever seen in real life, made even more arresting by that quiet, powerful confidence he has no matter what he does.

It takes me a bit to register that we've been standing in silence for quite some time now, and that he's studying me like he's concerned I've gone catatonic.

"Are you doing okay?" he asks worriedly. "Do you want me to drive you to the doctor to get checked out?"

Ah, yes, the fall. Let's go with that as the reason for all the staring.

"No, I'm fine. The way you held me until the adrenaline crash wore off actually helped immeasurably. Whole-body deep pressure has been known to do that. It's like how cattle are put in a squeeze chute to calm down when they get injections. That's actually what inspired therapeutic hug machines," I ramble on like some kind of runaway psychological encyclopedia.

"Took everything I had not to do *more* than just hold you," he admits in a low, heated growl.

The confession downright stuns me, and sends me on a freefall to dangerous depths unknown.

It's just the shock from earlier talking, I remind myself. He's saying things he shouldn't, and I'm interpreting it in ways I *really* shouldn't. All we need to do to get back to our status quo is change gears. Simple.

"Hey," I switch the subject then in a stroke of genius, drawing on a working theory I've always held about him. "What do you think about a little friendly climbing competition between you and me?"

His gaze instantly releases me from its magnetic hold. He blinks at me in surprise. "I'm listening," he says, the intrigue in his tone confirming my hypothesis: The man likes a challenge.

Between his affinity for climbing and his reputation for taking on bold investments that most of his billionaire colleagues won't touch, Logan thrives a bit on adventure. Which is why, while my brilliant intervention definitely changed the dynamic of our conversation, the air feels somehow even *more* charged now, in a new, different way I hadn't counted on. I back up to give myself some much-needed breathing room to articulate what I have in mind.

"I know you don't ever climb for speed," I explain. "And I don't either. But what do you think about doing a little speed test? Just for fun? Your brawn against my build." I may not have the reach or strength he does, but my being smaller also makes it possible for me to be considerably faster. It'll be an interesting match-up.

"Which wall?" he asks.

"I was thinking the Red Rock. First one to the top wins."

He arches an amused eyebrow at me. "And what happens when I win?"

Cocky bastard. At least he's not being all swoony and intense anymore. A bit of a lateral move, but I can work with it. "You forget, I've been climbing here almost every day for the last couple of years, while you've been mostly cooped up in offices and planes."

I say it teasingly, but the truth is, I can't remember the last time I saw him get a good climb in. Admittedly, this little challenge has a little something to do with that as well.

The man clearly misses it. I see it in his caged expression when he comes back here after one of his many meetings in the city, only to have to head straight to his office.

"You didn't answer my question," he says. "What do I get when I win?"

I really should be annoyed that he's not considering me a real climbing threat here, but oddly, I find his gruff confidence more entertaining than anything else. The man's fun to lock horns with. "I don't know. What do you want?" I toss back without thinking.

Big mistake.

I watch, almost mesmerized as he does some sort of Jedi mind trick on me, saying nothing and yet somehow getting me to blush. Then, a hazy minute later, he holds his hand out with a smile and I reach out to shake it—an automated response we're hardwired to do according to some interesting articles I read a while back.

Wait a sec. Did I just black out? Did I miss what his terms were?

From the way he's smiling and not letting me pull my hand back just yet, it's clear he knows the psychology behind handshakes as well. Damn him. "What did we just agree to?" I ask, more than a little nervously. "What does the winner get?"

His hand squeezes mine just a little bit firmer, and I feel him mentally tugging me in just a little bit closer.

"If I win," he says in a way that's somehow charmingly

arrogant, "I get the kiss I didn't take earlier when I was holding you."

He slowly lets my hand go, but still manages to keep me tethered to him by an invisible cord. "And if you win, you get the option to get out of it...but only if you can truly, honestly tell me that you don't want me to kiss you."

Holy crap.

See, *this* is why you should never do a deal with a billionaire.

The stakes are usually just way too high.

6

| LOGAN |

Close to a week later, I arrive at the gym after dropping off Hannah and see that Nicole's early again. She's waiting for me this time. I have no idea why that pleases me so fucking much, but it does.

I texted her last night to confirm we'd be doing our little climbing contest today. Only after my on-site doctor gave her a full medical work-up to make sure she didn't suffer any residual injuries from her fall, of course.

"So, did you get the results of my bloodwork and invasive body cavity search from Dr. Sings-While-He-Probes?" she grouses by way of greeting.

For a woman in a related medical field, it's funny to discover how difficult a patient she could be.

"Hello to you, too. And yes, you have the all-clear to climb today. Congrats."

Lordy, the woman has a spectacular glare.

At the door, I punch my security code in and ask

conversationally, "Ready to lose today, sweetheart?"

Swear to god, she looks ready to kick me in the balls.

When I see she's got Becca's keys this time—the neon pink pepper spray keychain is a dead giveaway—I motion for her to unlock the door and let us in. "Forgot your MP3 player in the car again?" I ask, wondering how early she got here this morning.

"No," she says simply, offering no further explanation.

Once inside, she heads off without another word to go get limbered up and I stay where I am for a few seconds longer to watch her feline grace from the back.

Pity I won't get that view when we're up on the wall together. Seeing as how I don't intend to fall behind her at any point during this climb.

She's right about the fact that she's been clocking in way more hours climbing than I have the last couple of years. And I know she's become a hell of a climber; I've watched her get stronger and more skilled with no small amount of admiration.

But, I've got one significant edge over her in this little competition.

I really want that fucking kiss.

On the main floor, I see my normal morning crew gathered at the Red Rock wall, *plus* about a dozen others who aren't scheduled.

That's when I realize Nicole's already in her rock

climbing shoes. *She was in here practicing.*

Not only did my own workers let her in here early, but even now, they're huddling around her feeding her different tips on how to beat me.

Traitors.

To be fair though, she probably used all her psychological witchery on them to get into their heads and on her side. Honestly, if the woman wasn't already very happy and successful in her career of choice, I'd hire her as my corporate negotiator. She's that good.

As we both stand before the wall, her studying the route she wants to take up, and me studying her, my workers start taking bets on who's going to win. I know my people love me; most of them have been with me since I opened the gym. But be that as it may, the bets are friggin' nine-to-one in *her* favor.

At the announcement of those odds, she quirks a brow at me and says with a simpering smile, "I'm *really* going to enjoy smacking you in the backside with my rappel ropes from the top."

Christ, she's just so damn cute.

"Let's do this." She reaches for a harness and pulls it on while I do the same. Her hands are quick and sure, but I'm still done before she is.

"One second," I say before she can reach for the wall.

I drop to my knees in front of her to tighten the straps around her thighs. The open form of the harness secures at the thigh and waist, but she left too much room on both like most people do.

"They don't have to be that snug," she protests and I glance up at her, realizing my face is practically buried between her legs.

She's lucky I was too focused on getting her properly geared up to notice earlier or I would've been sorely tempted to kick all my workers out of the gym and make *much* better use of our current position.

"They do need to be this snug," I inform her gruffly, as I stand up to tighten her waist straps the same way. "I'm not taking any chances with your safety."

She gazes at me for a second before reaching over to my harness straps, worriedly tugging on them to test their tension the way I did hers.

"Just checking," she says.

This damn woman and her bleeding heart.

"Ready?" calls out Derick.

We both nod.

"Go!"

She jumps at the wall, pulling herself up with quick, sure movements.

Shit, she's pretty fast.

Still, I pull ahead of her in two long reaches, climbing on feel alone. I never got into painting by numbers as a kid, and I never got in the habit of climbing by color-coded handholds either.

Not even a minute in and I'm officially having a grand fucking time. I've missed this. I'm not sure when I stopped focusing on Nicole and switched my attention over to just enjoying the hell out of the climb, but before I know it, we're at the halfway point.

I look over and do a double take, impressed that she's keeping pace with me.

"You're having fun," she says between slightly labored breaths, her eyes lighting up with pleasure over that fact.

It's like she's taken a seminar on how to make herself insanely adorable to me.

And now I'm back to giving her all my attention.

She's got her lower lip in her mouth and she's chewing on it in her concentration. I can see her motions slowing down a bit. It's the fatigue setting in. If I'm feeling it, she has to be also.

"You're doing great," I say. "But, you're using your forearms and biceps to pull you up too much for some of these angles. Push off more with your legs. You'll fatigue less that way."

"You're trying to help me win?" she asks, surprised.

"Nah, just trying to help you come in second."

I see her frame shake with laughter. "Stop distracting me."

Likewise. The woman's very existence is a distraction. And the thought of kissing the living daylights out of her later is starting to make my harness uncomfortable.

Dammit, dumbass, think of something else.

We fall into silence as we make our way past the three-quarter mark. She's a half a body length behind me now, and slowing down.

Nothing against her; she's in good shape, but this wall is punishing. Up this high, the holds are fewer and farther apart. Handling the gaps requires pushing your body past the ache, past the exhaustion, and keeping your mind sharp for each successive move you decide to make.

Speaking of keeping our minds sharp…mine gets sidetracked big time when I glance back at her once more and somehow manage to see straight down her fucking shirt.

And just like that, my hand misses the handhold I was going for. I adjust my feet and take a second to regroup. But, it's a second too long.

Nicole's beautiful backside glides right past my line of sight an instant before I hear her slap the top of the wall.

"Yes!" she hollers before rappelling down the wall. I reach up and tap the top of the wall before following her down, the sound of applause for Nicole's victory greeting my descent.

When my feet touch the ground, I immediately unbuckle my harness and clap her on the shoulder. "Good climb."

"You too," she says with a gracious smile.

I'm not sure whether to be insulted or entertained by the supreme relief I see in her eyes as I concede. But I know exactly how I feel about the way her gaze keeps dipping down to my mouth as if she just can't help herself.

That's when I call out for everyone to get back to opening up the gym, while none too subtly corralling her back to my office.

"Time to collect," I say as soon as the door is securely shut. And locked. "So, what's it going to be, Nicole? Do you want me to kiss you or not?"

7

| LOGAN |

"Wh—" She backs up a step. "But *I* won the race."

"Yes, you did." I say. "And what you won is the option to get out of the kiss if and only if you can tell me truthfully that you don't want me to kiss you."

I lean against the closed door and cross my arms over my chest, exuding a calm I'm definitely not feeling. "Well? What's it going to be? Do you *want* me to kiss you?"

She exhales slowly before meeting my eyes. "That's not a fair question."

"Sure, it is. All you need to do is tell the truth. If you don't want me to kiss you, just say so. But if you can't honestly make that statement, come here."

I want her to fucking come to me. I *need* to know that she wants this kiss as badly as I do.

"Just a kiss?" she asks softly.

Not wanting to spook her, I give her the tamest response I can, "Why? What else did you have in mind?"

Though she stifles it well, I can still see faint traces of amusement in her expression.

"You drive me crazy sometimes," she says with a sigh.

"Good thing you have professional training with that sort of thing."

"Stop being charming."

"No can do. We all need to play the hand we're dealt, beautiful."

The compliment seems to take her by surprise.

I have no idea why it would. The woman is gorgeous. Standing there with her mass of blonde curls done up in a tight braid per usual when she climbs. While I do prefer seeing her hair down, running in waves of dark gold and pale honey to her waist, that braid is pretty darn cute as well. Especially when the wispy curls start coming loose from her braid, turning into a halo of ringlets like the ones she's currently puffing out of her face.

I've never found adorable this damn sexy before.

As she continues to deliberate, I shove my hands in my pockets to keep from reaching for her. I don't want to persuade this decision out of her by touching her and showing her just how good it could be; she needs to get there all on her own.

Thank god, it looks like she's on her way.

Her steps are hesitant at first. Then almost cement-weighted when my hands settle on her soft hips.

Meanwhile, I'm shocked as hell I'm able to still be this patient right now.

"Can I kiss you any way I want?" she asks shyly, staring at my lips as she touches her own with her fingertips.

Jesus Christ.

"That would probably be best," I gravel out. "Because if you leave it up to me, there's a good chance my mouth will start down where they were when I was doing your harness straps, and then work its way up."

Her breathing halts altogether for a second...before the sexiest fucking sound ever slips past her lips.

I flex my fingers against her hips and bring her a little closer. I don't want to rush her but goddamn, I'm about to lose my mind.

"Nicole. Make your decision, baby. *Now* before I come totally unglued."

She goes up on her tip-toes then and gently, hesitantly, grazes her lips over mine.

My arms lock around her as I give up all pretense of patience. I fuse my mouth to hers and I swear, I can feel every shy touch of her tongue against mine stroking over my now rock-hard shaft as well.

Every passing second of the kiss quickly proves to be more memorable than the last.

And by the end, she fucking owns my mouth.

That's when she pulls back on a gasp and slips out of my arms. Somehow, I manage to keep my shit together and stay the hell where I am.

"Come back here," I say, sounding simply demanding, instead of all-out ravenous. I've never had to use my poker face and negotiating skills with a woman before. Glad I've been training for most of my business life for this moment.

Nicole's a smart woman though. She stays where she is and just studies me carefully. Like I'm a Rubik's Cube she's trying to figure out.

"Why does it feel like you're the one claiming a prize even though I'm the one who won today?" she queries, voice more breathless than piqued.

"Probably because we both know I didn't actually lose," I retort with a shrug.

Stomping forward a single step, she drills me with a caustic glare, somehow managing to still be beautiful even while looking like she wants to attack me. "*I* won, fair and square."

Competitive little thing. "You sure about that, sweetheart? Because having your lips on mine feels a whole lot like winning to me."

She blushes. "You're impossible."

"Which you find charming." I grin. "You already admitted it."

"I'm leaving."

My grin fades. "Why? The prize-collecting isn't over yet."

She gives me a curious look. "Yes, it is."

Not by a longshot. I'm nowhere *near* done kissing this woman. "Have dinner with me tonight."

Wide, rounded sage green eyes blink up at me in shock. "I-I can't."

"Why not?"

"Because Hannah wants to go climbing first thing tomorrow morning."

Well, that effectively shifts the mood. "I know. She told me."

"So, I don't want to stay out late."

That she's already thinking a dinner with me will end late has my imagination spinning into overdrive.

"Raincheck then?" I ask. "For a night that you *can* 'stay out late?'"

She hesitates. "Maybe."

Maddening woman.

Turning to eye the exit, she says, "I'll be here tomorrow to start working with Hannah. Early, before the weekend rush." Then she scurries off.

I watch her go, surprised by how fiercely I dislike seeing her leave now.

8

| LOGAN |

After the exhausting night I just had, seeing Nicole outside of the gym bright and early this morning is a sight for sore eyes.

I don't even mind that she's got Derick's keys again.

"'Morning," she calls out with a smile that leaves her face as quickly as it appears. "Logan, what's wrong? You look awful."

That's an understatement. "Hannah caught some kind of stomach bug and was up all night crying and throwing up."

"Oh my god. Is she feeling better today?"

"A little. She finally stopped puking her guts up around two this morning. She's been sleeping ever since. My mom came over to stay with her early this morning since I had a bunch of international calls I needed to be on. I checked on her before I left and her fever was gone so that's something."

I punch in my security code and when Nicole unlocks the door, I prop it open with my foot but stop her from entering. Derick waves at us from the front desk. I grab his keys from her hand and toss them over to him. Then I pull her back outside and shut the door behind us.

"We have to reschedule Hannah's first climb for when she's feeling better," I tell her.

"Of course. Just let me know when." She places a gentle hand on my shoulder. "You should go home and get some rest while your mom is watching Hannah."

"I'm heading back now. I just came down here to tell you we couldn't make it."

"You could've just called or texted. I get up early."

"But then I wouldn't have been able to see you," I say simply, turning so my hands are flat against the wall on either side of her. "What are your plans for today?"

She shrugs. "I'd blocked off a couple of hours for Hannah, so nothing now in the morning. I've got a group outdoor climb after lunch, but other than that, it's an easy day."

"Good," I say, grazing my thumb over the darkened circles under her eyes. "I don't like seeing you this tired. You've been working too hard lately."

"Not really. I'm way busier in the summers. Although, I did get a wave of new clients recently. And I do have one client who's been having a really rough time with things so I've been squeezing in a ton of extra sessions for him. Oh, there's also those online seminars I'm teaching."

She smiles sheepishly. "Guess maybe my weeks *have* been a little busier than usual."

We're like two overworking peas in a pod.

She gazes up at me with a curious expression then. "Can I ask you something?"

"Sure."

"You didn't throw the race yesterday, did you?"

"Nope," I assure her. "I'm competitive as hell. I went all out."

"Then what happened? Folks said they saw you miss a handhold."

I sigh. May as well 'fess up. "When I looked back to see where you were on the wall, I saw down your shirt a little…okay, a lot."

At her startled expression, I lift an unapologetic shoulder, "What can I say? I'm a red-blooded guy. And you've got a pretty dynamite rack."

I expect her to be indignant and slap me. But instead, she just laughs. And flushes bright red.

"Why the blush?" I ask, running the backs of my knuckles over her warmed cheeks.

"I got a little distracted on the wall myself…when you passed me."

She mimics my half-shrug and gives me a playful smile. "What can I say? I'm a woman with two functioning eyes. And you've got a pretty dynamite tush."

Unable to stop myself, I steal a laughing kiss from her simpering lips. Why I've waited this long to spend time with the entertaining creature is beyond me.

"Are you going to keep collecting kisses from me even though you lost the challenge?" she asks as I push back from the wall.

"You're lucky that's all I'm collecting, sweetheart."

Her breath catches in her throat for a beat, before she recovers and says, "You do remember that you didn't win, right?"

"What I remember is our agreement that *if* you don't want me to do something, all you have to do is be completely honest about it," I counter.

Placing a hand on the small of her back I pull her off the wall so I can walk her over to her SUV. "Let's practice," I offer magnanimously. "Say, '*Logan, I don't want you to do anything more than kiss me.*' But, again, only if you really, really mean it."

I press her back against her driver's side door and cage her in once more. "Well?"

She stares at me with wide eyes. But says nothing.

Hot damn.

"We shouldn't," she says weakly.

I exhale slowly. "I'm well aware."

"B-but...I...want to. Do more, that is."

"So we're in agreement."

We stand there staring at each other in a stalemate

until my chirping phone interrupts the dangerous turn our conversation is taking. I check my text messages. "I need to run to the pharmacy and grab some more electrolytes for Hannah."

"Oh! Of course. Go, go." Nicole quickly turns to open her door. "Wait, do you need me to do that? You can head on home to be with her and I can go to the store for you guys."

"No, that's okay. My mom said she's still sleeping. And my pharmacy has a drive-thru so it'll be quick. You need to go home and take it easy before your outdoor climb."

I wait till she's buckled in before closing her door for her. When she rolls down her window, I duck in to steal another kiss. Longer this time.

Hell, kissing the sweet woman is quickly starting to become an addiction.

"Just so you know, we're not done talking about this," I say against her lips before stepping back to head over to my own car.

The look in her eyes as she nods sticks with me the entire drive to the pharmacy.

A half hour later, I'm hanging up my keys and walking over to Hannah's room to check on her. I place my hand against her forehead to make sure her fever hasn't come back.

My saint of a mother peeks in from the hallway. "I

think the worst is over."

I follow her into the living room and drop down on the couch tiredly. "Thanks for coming over this morning, Mom. If you need to get going, we'll be fine."

At her silence, I look over at her and find her smiling in that quintessential Mom way that tells me she's gearing up to do some pretty heavy meddling. "What's with the look?"

"You met someone, didn't you?"

Yet more proof that the woman is either part psychic or part witch. Been seeing evidence of it all my life. I shake my head in denial.

"Don't you dare lie to your mother," she scolds. "You've been different the last week or so. Don't bother denying it."

Did I mention she's also a human lie detector? It's no wonder I kept on the straight and narrow growing up. "Why the interrogation all of a sudden? You've never asked about the women I see before," I deflect to try and throw her off my scent.

"That's because none of them have been worth asking about," she says plainly.

And folks think I get my bluntness from my dad.

"Nothing's changed," I tell her. "Hannah is still my first priority. Dating anyone seriously isn't even on my radar."

Her smile disappears, and gets replaced with a

concerned headshake. "Honey, I know losing Janine was hard—"

"This isn't about that," I cut in.

It really isn't.

"Then why don't you give this one a chance to *become* serious? If she's affecting you this much, she must be special."

She is.

Thankfully, the sound of someone pulling into the front driveway provides me a much-appreciated escape from the conversation.

"I'll go see who that is." I head over to answer the doorbell and do a double take when I see Nicole standing on my porch.

"Hey," she says, waving.

Can't help it, simply seeing the woman makes me smile.

And just like that, the door is yanked wide open by my nosy mother.

"Where are your manners, Logan? Don't leave the woman standing out there in the cold. Come in, dear. I'm Logan's mother. And you are?"

Nicole backs up a slightly overwhelmed step. "Oh! Hello. I'm Nicole. Actually, no need to invite me in. I just came over to drop off some soup for Hannah. I had the stomach flu once, and this soup did wonders for me. It's the ginger and pumpkin in it."

She holds out a to-go soup container, which, of course, my mother intercepts with one hand, while basically dragging Nicole into the house with the other.

"Well, aren't you considerate? Come in for a bit." My mother is insistent.

I shoot Nicole a look that says, *'Run. Flee. Get out while you still can.'*

A slap upside my head puts a quick end to that.

Nicole smothers back a chuckle and comes inside fully. Eagerly now.

Great. Maybe *I'm* the one who should flee.

"Are you sure I'm not imposing, Mrs. Reynolds?"

My mom points at the nearest dining chair. "Sit, sit. And please, call me Carol."

"Thank you." Nicole smiles warmly before blinking in surprise. "Oh wow, Hannah's the spitting image of you. She has your eyes. I always assumed she got that from her mother since they're so different from Logan's…"

When her sentence trails off, I glance over to see her covering her mouth with her fingers, and looking downright uncomfortable.

No doubt because this is the first time Janine has come up between us in the entire five years since she first started coming to the gym.

For once, my mom is none the wiser as to what's going on. She chuckles over Nicole's observation. "I'd like to take credit for Hannah's beautiful hazel eyes, but she definitely got those from her mother Janine. Lovely girl. We were all devastated when she passed away."

"Mom," I interrupt, knowing this just got extra awkward for at least two of us in the room. "Nicole has to work today. She can't stay."

I send Nicole a silent apology with my eyes, which she mirrors right back.

"My goodness." My mom stops fussing suddenly and stares at the two of us. "I remember you now. You were one of Janine's bridesmaids, weren't you?"

I hear a startled sound come from the living room and turn to find Hannah standing there looking at Nicole like she's never seen her before. "Wait, you knew my mother?"

Shit.

9

| NICOLE |

"Hannah, what are you doing out of bed, dear?" Carol immediately goes over to try and usher her back upstairs, giving me a brief second to sneak a peek over at Logan.

His attention is wholly focused on Hannah, concern etched into his features.

"Oh my gosh, Dad, why didn't you tell me Nicole knew Mom?" Fortunately, she doesn't actually wait for an answer, choosing instead to run over to sit on the seat beside me. "Did you go to high school with them, too?"

I shake my head. "No, I met your mom in college. We were dorm mates."

"That's so cool. So, you guys were close." She rolls her eyes. "Well, duh, of course you were. You were a bridesmaid." Jumping up excitedly, she claps her hands and runs over to a nearby display cabinet. "That means you were in the wedding photos."

Before she can make it all the way to the cabinet, however, Hannah stops suddenly to grip the kitchen counter, face pale as a ghost, eyes shut tight.

"Hannah!" I rush forward with Carol and Logan right on my tail.

"I'm okay." She opens her eyes slowly, her coloring tinged with green. "I just got super dizzy."

Logan quickly scoops her up into his arms. "That's because you're supposed to be in bed, missy. You had a rough night."

"But, I'm hungry," replies Hannah, frowning. "And a little bored."

Logan perches Hannah on one hip and reaches for the soup container I brought. "Nicole has some soup for you." He places it on a tray with a spoon and a bottle of Gatorade. "You can eat the soup in bed and watch a movie on my iPad. But no more coming downstairs, you hear me, squirt? I don't want you taking a tumble. Next time, you call me if you need anything. I'll be your personal butler until you're feeling better."

"Can my butler bring me ice cream instead?" she negotiates with big, beseeching eyes like the fabulous nine-year-old she is. "Folks on TV always eat ice cream when they're sick."

"If you want to have another projectile vomiting fiesta, sure," says Logan matter-of-factly.

His mother and I stifle a chuckle when Hannah groans

and slaps a hand over her mouth. "Never mind," she squeaks. "Soup is good."

"You sure?" prods Logan never breaking form as he carries her up the stairs. "We could put sprinkles on the ice cream to make the vomit really extra colorful this time."

"Dad! Gross!"

He continues this all the way until they're out of earshot.

I shake my head. "He's so great with her."

"That he is," agrees Carol.

I turn to face her. "It's nice to see you again, Carol. I know we only spoke a couple of times at the wedding and rehearsal dinner. I didn't think you'd remember me."

"Oh, I never forget a face, dear."

Yeah, I *really* should've heeded Logan's silent advice to escape when I had the chance.

"So…you and my son?"

"Are friends," I fill in firmly.

"And yet, this is the first I'm hearing about you since Hannah was born."

The reason why that is crashes over me like a wave of shame.

I first met Janine during freshman orientation back at Stanford. We'd hit it off immediately and gotten pretty close that year. So much so that we decided to room together the following year.

While I'd never had a *best* friend—my parents

thought it silly and unnecessary to analyze or measure friendship on a scale in that way—Janine was definitely the closest thing I had to it.

That said, when she and Logan got pregnant during our junior year and she told me she wouldn't be coming back to finish her degree, I admit, I could've been a better friend to her. I *should've* told her that being a mom was of course more important than getting her business degree like she'd always wanted.

But I didn't.

I believe my exact words were that it'd be a 'waste' for her not to complete her schooling.

I don't know that I'll ever forgive myself for saying that.

Not that it's any excuse, but I can honestly say I didn't know better back then. It's what I was raised to understand was important. Both my parents were accomplished scientists with a ton of initials after their names. I never grew up seeing my finger paintings or gold star work on the fridge. It was always their accomplishments they made a fuss over, their life in academia they discussed. To show me what to aspire to, what was important.

I wasn't taught otherwise until the day Janine didn't wake up after her emergency C-section. That was the day I learned what was *really* important.

"I don't think Logan ever forgave me for what I said to Janine," I tell Carol.

"There's nothing to forgive," says Logan from the bottom of the staircase. "A lot of other folks told her the same thing."

I can hear in his voice that he's being truthful. Which makes me thoroughly confused. All this time, I thought the reason why he'd kept his distance from me was because he hated me for what I'd said.

"But—" I stare back at him, wanting to understand, but not wanting to dredge up old memories for him.

"I wasn't thrilled you'd said that to Janine. But I understood. Janine was honestly better in business school than I was," he explains with a wistful smile, which quickly transforms into a deadly serious stare. "The only thing I *won't* forgive is if I find out *Hannah* ever hears what you said. That's the reason why I've kept our past swept under a rug all this time. To make certain she doesn't."

Oh. Jesus, that makes sense.

He drills me with a hard look. "I *never* want my little girl to think her birth was anything but a gift that everyone we knew was ecstatic and supportive of. Do you hear me? What I just told her upstairs is that you got busy with your last year of college and grad school so we simply lost touch after her mother died. I know you don't like to lie, but none of that is untruthful. So that's all she needs to ever know about this topic. Are we clear?"

Crystal. "You have my word."

He points a stern finger at me. "And you can't go all

shrinky about this stuff. Okay?"

I tilt my head sympathetically. "Logan, I think you and I both know I can't possibly promise such a thing."

Carol bursts out laughing. "Oh, my. You're a fun one."

The genuine approval in her tone is a welcome surprise. I'd only met Logan's parents briefly, but I do remember how similar they'd been to Janine's parents. Warm, nurturing, openly affectionate.

All the things my parents weren't.

I still remember the night I'd stayed over at Janine's parents' home a couple days before the wedding along with Janine and the other bridesmaids. I'd never gone to a sleepover before that, and truth be told, it was a bit like staying up all night with a bunch of aliens...in the coziest little cottage imaginable.

To me, that cottage had been fairytale perfect. The other bridesmaids had been gossiping about how Logan had offered to buy Janine's parents a mansion as a reverse wedding gift, and how crazy it was that they'd turned down his generous offer.

Meanwhile, I'd spent the night walking around, cataloging all the homey smells wafting from the kitchen, all the old crayon scribbles on the walls, and all the family photos proudly displayed on every available surface.

That cottage had been a true home, not just a house like the one I grew up in.

And it was clear Janine had been a well-loved child, not just an offspring like I'd been.

The day Janine passed away, I remember screaming inside at the universe for being so paradoxically unfair. For not even letting her see her child. A child I knew without a doubt she'd already loved more than my parents had ever loved me.

I'm fairly certain that moment was when the old Nicole died. Right there in the hospital alongside her friend.

Given the trajectory of my own life before that moment, I'd been on track to end up like my parents, I'm sure, focused more on a lasting legacy than a strong family.

A home, not just a house...

Children, not just offspring...

A family, not a legacy...

Janine's chance to have all that had been stolen from her; I didn't want ignorance to keep me from mine.

After that, my metamorphosis progressed pretty quickly.

For one, I switched my major to psychology—much to my parents' disdain. They never were a fan of the social sciences. Not surprisingly, they haven't talked to me much since.

I imagine they'd hate knowing I was spending most of my days in a climbing gym instead of in a lab or a lecture hall. But, I wouldn't have my life any other way. Climbing helped transform my career and *me* in more ways than I can count.

In that sense, stumbling upon Logan's gym while I was doing my post-grad training had been pure kismet. I'd had no idea he'd started a climbing franchise, let alone the biggest, most successful one in the state. Like he said, we'd lost touch completely. In fact, it wasn't until a few weeks after I'd gotten my membership and started seriously considering using it for therapy sessions when I first ran into him.

He didn't speak to me that first day, and I didn't blame him for not wanting to. It took a while, but eventually, he did talk to me. Sort of. He gave me pointers on my climbing at least, nothing more. We didn't bring up the past; we didn't chitchat. I could tell he thought I was strange. But, over time, things went from awkward to civil. And then from cordial to what it is now.

And in that time, I've watched him be an incredible dad to Hannah. Janine would've been so proud. If she were still alive today, I have no doubt in my mind that the pair would be one of those perfect power parenting couples all of us mere mortals aspire to become.

I gaze sadly at the memorial of Janine over the mantle next to the dining room, lovingly adorned with artwork Hannah had made for her over the years.

"Janine would've been such a wonderful mother to Hannah," I whisper then, voicing the thoughts I've long held.

Feeling Carol's eyes on me, I turn back to her and smile. "The kind of mother you were to Logan, I'm sure...the kind of strong female role model every kid deserves."

"Mom," says Logan, breaking the silence that follows. "Did Nicole tell you that she works with students in her therapy practice?"

I feel like he's defending me. And I don't feel worthy of it. At least the old Nicole doesn't.

His jaw is locked, his expression firm, brooking no argument. "Nicole is amazing with them. I've admired her for years. What she's able to accomplish with those kids, I've never seen anything like it before."

I blink, startled.

"That's why she's the *only* person outside of family I'd ever entrust Hannah's safety to."

10

| NICOLE |

"Well, that's quite the character reference," says Carol, pulling me out of the trance that Logan's words had put me in. "You must be quite the psychologist."

"I'm a therapist, actually, specializing in experiential therapy, which basically focuses more on doing rather than talking."

"How fascinating. And you work with young children?"

"More teens and pre-teens. After my master's, I applied for a part-time resource position with the public school system here. They assigned me to travel to middle schools and high schools all across the district three days a week to counsel students having difficulties. And I've been re-upping that temp contract ever since."

How could I not? I get to help students learn how to build themselves up when they felt low, make themselves feel whole again even if they've never known the feeling.

Next to climbing, it's the best feeling ever.

I smile, reminiscing about how I got started. "I actually first decided to start a tiny private practice partly *so* I could keep my part-time job, funnily enough. Mostly college and homeschool kids on the days I wasn't doing school visits. But then, most of my other students started coming in afterschool and on the weekends to try my climbing-based sessions outdoors and at Logan's gym. After that, my practice just took off."

As I talk, Logan stands off to the side, observing me intently the entire time. It's unnerving. The man has always had this *presence* about him that takes him from merely handsome to devastatingly striking.

Oy, what an entirely inappropriate observation to be making at the moment.

I quickly return to the topic at hand. "I actually have Logan to thank for a lot of my success," I inform Carol. "He actually waives the membership fees for the students who do therapy sessions with me."

Carol nods approvingly at her son. "Good boy." She goes over and pats him on the head. "Your mother raised you right."

Logan rolls his eyes.

I chuckle.

It's no wonder he's such a great dad.

I fully prescribe to the notion of nurture over nature. And since it's more than evident that his mere existence is one of the highlights of his parents' lives, the fact that he raises Hannah in the same fashion is no surprise.

I can honestly say I've never met a parent who actually misses their kid quite so much when they're at their grandparents, not the way Logan does. Though it's only one weekend night a week, I've seen the man get seriously bummed out when she's not around.

It's almost unbearably swoonworthy to witness.

Carol grabs the chair next to me. "So, I take it you're helping Hannah with her bullying problem?"

"Not directly, no. And not officially, either. I simply volunteered to work with her a bit."

"Twisted my arm is more accurate," chimes in Logan from the kitchen.

Carol pats me on the hand. "Well, I'm glad you did. Hannah just hasn't been the same since the incident. She was always painfully shy in public to begin with, but after that horrifying prank those awful older kids did to her, she definitely became more withdrawn."

Shaking her head with disgust, she adds angrily, "Personally, I think the students getting expelled wasn't nearly a harsh enough punishment. They didn't even know her. They only targeted Hannah because her father's a billionaire; what a ridiculous reason to torment a child."

I do a double take. Logan failed to mention that very important detail. Now I understand why it was so hard for him to talk to me about it.

"Hang on." Carol peers over at Logan in astonishment. "Are you actually going to let Hannah climb as part of her therapy with Nicole?"

"It isn't therapy," Logan and I say in unison.

"And yes," he answers. "I am going to let her climb. If she wants to."

"How exciting. Can Phil and I come by to watch? When will it be? After school?"

"The weekend would be better," says Logan.

"Then that narrows it down to a Saturday," I tell Carol. "I have a strict no-work policy on Sundays."

"Oh, do you go to church, dear?"

"If you consider the NFL a religion, sure." I grin.

Logan lets out a surprised chuckle. "You're preaching to the right choir with this family. Hannah's been watching football with me since she was born."

"Lucky girl. I only started in college, but I've been a diehard San Fran fanatic ever since."

"So, you're a 49ers fan," says Logan. "Hmm."

I'm not liking the sound of that. "Aren't you?" I ask, in a tone that clearly states any response other than 'hell yes' is totally unacceptable.

"Sorry, I've been a Broncos fan since birth."

I think my ears may be bleeding. "But you grew up in the Bay Area just like I did."

"We only moved out here to California when I was in grade school. My dad's originally from Colorado, making me a second-generation Broncos fan." He grins. "And Hannah a third."

"You mean you're brainwashing your child to support an inferior team?" The poor girl.

"You do realize the Broncos have been to more Super Bowls than the 49ers," he argues, looking thoroughly entertained over how huffy I'm getting.

"But San Fran has *won* more Super Bowls," I throw back at him. "Which only proves your team is better at losing."

"At least we won our last time at the Super Bowl. How did the last one work out for you guys again?"

I glare at him. "You're pissing me off. And I don't need that kind of negative energy going into a climb. So, no more talking for the next…" I mentally check my gym schedule. "Twenty-two hours."

"Interesting. Can't go a whole twenty-four without talking to me, huh?"

I stay true to my radio silence, refusing to let him goad me. All the while, my heart is starting to thump a little faster in my chest. I'm not used to this teasing side of him. It's dangerous, unchartered. And so freaking fun.

As he continues to stare at me in amusement, I determinedly bat away the butterflies taking flight in my belly and thank Carol for the lovely visit, pointedly giving Logan my back the entire time. Much to his visible enjoyment.

As I drive over from Logan's home to the climb site where I'm meeting my group, I ponder his question. Now that I've been talking to the man regularly, truthfully, I don't believe I'd enjoy not being able to talk to him for an entire day.

Not that there's any way I'm going to admit such a thing to a *Broncos* fan.

11

| LOGAN |

I should've rescheduled this site visit.

With the construction for my newest U.S. climbing gym in Vegas in its final phase, I know it's important that I be here since I'm a stickler for details. But, frankly, both my focus and my mood has been shit the entire time.

It's no big secret that I'm not a fan of traveling. It's always been a hard rule of mine not to go out of town more than a few days at a time and never two weeks in a row. Dad first, billionaire second. Always.

The folks I do business with complain at times that I'm difficult to work with as a result, but I don't give a damn. What's the point in being successful if I can't prioritize my life as a dad?

What I'm finding vastly less tolerable about this trip, however, is that I'm not just missing my kid, I'm also missing the hell out of a certain shrink who's been slowly driving me to distraction over the past couple of weeks.

As I've come to discover, my days are pretty fucking boring whenever Nicole's not around to make me crazy. And vice versa. I miss getting her all worked up, teasing her about her precious 49ers. Christ, I think I even miss hearing all her cute psychobabble.

Yep, I've got it bad. But, strangely, I'm okay with that. The woman hasn't just gotten under my skin and into my head, she's actually starting to fit into my *life*. It's kind of shocking that the universe isn't combusting as a result.

Up until now, a person would need to undergo a federal-level background screening and successfully pass the equivalent of multiple years of advanced ivy league training and both written and field tests in any subject of my choosing to even *qualify* to have a microscopic role in my daughter's life.

Curiously enough, no one's ever made the cut.

Nicole, however, in all her weird and head-shrinking glory, managed to leapfrog over my very strict requirements and somehow become a fairly constant fixture.

Impressive, really.

I confess, I'd had my doubts. But, it's actually been going really well. She doesn't have Hannah looking at inkblots and talking about her feelings all the time or anything like that. No, the pair just hang out regularly, tackling projects together or doing stuff outdoors.

And as of last week, they've also been climbing.

For Hannah's first climb, I kid you not, I made sure

the entire climbing area was blocked off with barricade tape and three of my workers were on the wall with her the entire time.

Nicole indulged me since it was her first climb (and maybe also because I'd threatened to revoke her membership if she didn't). For Hannah's second climb this week, however, she insisted it would have to be just her and Hannah up there, no interference, no hovering. Period. I grudgingly agreed, mainly because Hannah puppy-dog-eyed me.

But then this site visit in Vegas got penciled into my schedule right at the same time. When I couldn't postpone it, I made sure to warn my entire staff to keep a close eye on them while I was gone. Every worker in the place received orders to grab the on-site physician for even the littlest knee scrape.

On *either* of them.

Swear to god, if Nicole hadn't sent me the link to a live feed of Hannah's climb earlier today, I would've been useless all afternoon.

I'd been nervous as hell to watch it, but admittedly, it was pretty damn amazing to see my little girl in the video owning that wall like a tiny little badass and having the time of her life.

The fact that Nicole had made a point to arrange the recording and live feed for me today without me even asking (aka demanding) is yet another reason why I can't stop thinking about the woman.

Her sweetness could possibly be her sexiest quality.

I know it's late and Nicole's probably in bed already, but I have this strange need to talk to her. Thank her for the video. Hell, just hear her voice, even.

Normally, just getting to chat with Hannah before she goes to sleep is enough to make my trips more bearable. But the last couple of nights, I've needed something more.

I've needed my Nicole fix.

And just like that, it's as if my phone dials itself.

"Hello?" Nicole's voice on the other end is low and sleepy, but also curled around a faint, very distinguishable purr of pleasure.

Instantly, I'm as hard as a rock.

"What were you just doing?" I ask.

"Logan?"

"Are there any other men calling you in the middle of the night?" There better not fucking be any.

"Of course not."

"Then back to my question. Did I interrupt something?" I ask, already enjoying the hell out of this call.

"Just getting ready for bed," she replies innocently.

I'm not going to let her get off that easily. My cock is practically leaking precum already, I'm so fucking turned on. "You were touching yourself," I say and I hear her gasp on the other end. "Were you thinking about me?" I want to hear her say it.

"I...should probably just talk to you when you get back." Her voice breaks.

Jesus, she's touching herself right now.

"Did you already come or did I interrupt you before you got a chance to?" I ask, and I swear I can *hear* her blush.

"You...interrupted me," she admits, her voice a tortured whisper that sends a pulse of electricity straight to my balls.

"Tell me what you were thinking about while you were trying to make yourself come. What was I doing? Was I sucking on your clit? Fucking your tight pussy from behind?"

Dammit, if she moans like that one more time...

"S-something else..." she says almost too quietly for me to hear. "I-I was...on my knees."

Oh, fuck.

I squeeze my eyes closed and feel my cock throb in my hand. Sure, I'd wanted to know what gets her hot. But knowing that she was thinking about sucking my dick is killing me.

"I want to hear you come. Right here on the phone with me," I say and she whimpers.

I can hear it, she's almost at the end of her tether.

"Logan, I shouldn't."

"But you *will*."

The sexiest sound of defiance escapes her throat in

response to my dictate and my imagination automatically takes over, putting me right there with the feisty creature. My brain can almost see her hypnotic green eyes right now, challenging me at every turn while her slender fingers play with her perfect little pussy.

"Come for me on the phone, and I'll make you come in person when I see you next."

That breaks her.

I don't think she can even hear me anymore. She sounds utterly lost in her own world of soft moans and breathless pleasure.

Christ. I'm going to come in my hand at this rate. I've never had phone sex before and honestly, I didn't think it'd do it for me.

But goddamn, this is fucking doing it for me.

A sudden wave of primal possession washes over me then as I listen to her come her brains out. "Have you ever come on the phone before?" I demand gruffly after she's had a chance to catch her breath.

Even if I hate the answer, I want to, *need to* know if she's done this with someone else.

"N-no. Never," she says.

The tightness in my chest eases a bit. But not fully. There's only one thing that'll make that happen. "I'm the only one who gets to make you come on the phone. Me. No other fucking guy." *Ever.* "Say it."

I don't know why I feel part caveman around this

woman, but I can't seem to control it.

I let go of my cock and sit up. "I need to hear you say it, Nicole. No other guy gets to make you come. Not on the phone. For damn sure not anywhere else."

"If you're asking if I'm the kind of woman who has casual things with different men at the same time, I'm not."

Yeah, that's not enough. I want to *know* that when she's with me, no other men even register on her radar. Lord knows that's the case for me. Ever since Nicole wormed her way into my world, I don't notice any other women. And I sure as hell don't want her noticing any other men.

"I only want you, Nicole. And I want to hear that you only want me, too."

"But we haven't even..." she says softly. "It's way too early for us to—"

"We've known each other for years," I break into her objection. If I'm being honest with myself, she's been under my skin since the first day I saw her in my gym five years ago. "So, no, it's not too early."

It's long overdue if you ask me. And I'm going to make up for lost time. "*Do* you want any other guys?" I ask plainly, doing my best to mute the growl resulting from the very idea of that.

"No, Logan. Just you."

"Good." I wrap my fist around my hard dick again. "Now, let me hear you come for me again. Give me something beautiful to listen to while I'm pumping my cock dry thinking about you."

The command draws a startled, ragged whimper out of her. Followed by the unmistakable sounds of a sweet, surprise aftershock orgasm.

Knowing my words got her there is enough to *almost* send me over the edge. But I stop myself before I do. I'm going to need an ice-cold shower after this, but I don't care. I don't want to come without being able to see her. Touch her. Fucking taste her.

Her breathing eventually returns back to normal, and then slowly starts to drift off.

"You falling asleep on me, baby?"

"A little. Sorry. Although, really, you only have yourself to blame."

So damn cute when she's punchy. "Do you have lunch plans for tomorrow?"

"I thought you don't come back until night time," she murmurs sleepily.

"I'm going to change my flight schedule. You going to be free to have lunch with me?"

"Actually, I am," she says, her voice clearly smiling. It's faint, shy. But it's there. Dammit, I should've video-called her so I could see it. Next trip, for sure.

"What do you want to eat?" she asks.

That's easy. "You. Be ready at noon."

12

| LOGAN |

She isn't ready at noon.

I got her text that she's running late on my drive from the airport so I head over to the gym instead of her place like we'd planned...only to find her *still* on the wall with that Kenny kid.

It's not that I'm being possessive of my time with her—okay, maybe it's that a little—but I don't like the idea of anyone taking advantage of her. Her bleeding heart is one of the things I respect the most about her. And if I have to have a little intervention with anyone who isn't showing said bleeding heart the same kind of respect, I damn well will.

"Everything going okay here?" I ask, greeting the pair as they finally make their descent.

Nicole turns to give me a smile that lights up the whole fucking room.

Kenny, on the other hand, looks less than thrilled to

see me. He gives me a cursory nod and turns back to Nicole. "One more climb? Last one, I swear."

"Kenny, your session finished two hours ago." Though she looks pained in doing so, she holds her ground. "I'll see you next week for your next session, okay? You did really well today."

Kenny shoots me an annoyed look. "Fine. Whatever. See you around."

And then he stomps off, looking ready to throw a tantrum. Seriously, that kid needs to learn some friggin' manners. For a six-foot college freshman, he's acting like a spoiled two-year old.

"You okay, sweetheart?" I ask her, concerned with the heavy sigh I hear her expel.

"I'm fine. Just…long day."

Normally, I'd ask any person who looked like this if they wanted to talk about it, but knowing that Nicole literally can't because of confidentiality, I go straight to the making her feel better part. "C'mon. Let's go up to my office. I think you need a shoulder rub and sleep. You can take a power nap on my couch before your next session."

"God, that sounds amazing. What about our lunch date though? You must be hungry."

"Starving," I agree. "But I already told you what I wanted to eat. And you sleeping while I'm eating your pussy isn't going to work for me."

Her cheeks go scarlet. "I thought you were joking."

"I'd never joke about making you come, sweetheart. Now, you need me to carry you upstairs?"

"Lordy at this rate, yes."

I swiftly scoop her up and begin walking over to my office like I'm carrying her over the threshold.

"Logan! Put me down," she laughs. "I wasn't serious."

"Quit squirming, woman. You're getting my cock all excited."

Oh, shit.

She looks far too pleased with that admission.

Sure enough, she shifts to snuggle more into my arms so she can not-so-innocently rub that perfect ass of hers against my now rock hard dick.

I practically sprint the rest of the way to my office.

Jesus, she feels good in my arms, and from what I can tell from the way she's breathing, her little upright lap dance had an effect on her as well.

"Still need that nap, baby? Or are you going to let me taste that sweet pussy that's been torturing my cock?"

She ducks her face against my neck to keep her burning hot cheeks hidden as she says quietly, "Not tired anymore."

So ridiculously adorable. And for some reason, that turns me on even more.

Only one problem.

Why in the hell didn't I install some damn blinds in

my office?

I meant what I said earlier. I'm starving for this woman. If I don't fucking taste her pussy soon, I'm going to become unhinged.

The only option for privacy in here would be my private bathroom and that's totally unacceptable. I'm not making Nicole come for me for the first time on a restroom sink.

Shit. This isn't going to happen.

Defeated, I place her gently down on the couch. "Change of plans. Why don't you go on and take that nap? I'll be right back."

She frowns. "Wait, where are you going?"

"Down to the locker rooms to take a cold shower."

Her gaze shoots down to the front of my jeans.

Before I even realize her intent, she's got my jeans undone and her warm, soft hand stroking the head of my cock.

"Nicole, we can't."

She holds my gaze. "We could go to your storage room."

Tempting. So fucking tempting.

She rubs her thumb across the tip, and slowly starts pumping her other hand along my shaft.

Hell, she wins.

I grab her wrist and pull her up to her feet, zipping my jeans back up as I propel her out the door and into the storage area directly next to my office.

"You need to be quiet while I'm making you come," I say as I lock the door behind us, all the while hoping she won't be *too* quiet. After hearing what she sounds like when she comes on the phone, a live show today would make my fucking day.

She frowns. "But you already made me come. Twice, in fact. So," she says in a mind-messing mix of shy and feisty, "I'm thinking I owe you."

This woman is going to drive me insane.

"No, not today." I push her gently back against the wall, needing to feel her, taste her. Something. Anything.

"You're being bossier than usual."

I think she means that to be a complaint, but with my hands currently under her shirt pinching her tight nipples, it comes out as a breathy moan.

"You like when I'm bossy."

"Sometimes. But you had your turn on the phone last night. I want *you* to come this time." With that, she drops to her knees. "In my mouth."

Jesus Christ.

How many times have I fantasized about this? About how my dick would look between those soft, sweet lips of hers as she stares up at me with those big green eyes and makes me come so hard I nearly black out.

My cock pulses and starts downright *throbbing* at the visual.

I know she doesn't like how demanding I can get, and truth be told, it's sexy as hell when she's all bold and assertive like this. But, I can't let her. At least not until I've had her come on my cock a couple dozen times. After that, sure.

She reads my expression like a book. "You don't want me in control, do you?" she asks, incredulous.

"Next time," I offer gruffly as a compromise.

She stares up at me for a beat before reaching for my hands and guiding me to spear them through her hair. I tighten my fingers against her scalp while she slowly undoes my jeans again.

Jesus, this woman is like a fantasy.

"Are you sure?" I ask, feeling a serious lack of blood flow to my brain. In my experience, women don't really like having their mouths fucked like this.

"I'm sure," she says before testing my hold on her and shivering when I tug her hair just enough as her lips tease my tip.

Hell, that first wet glide of her tongue along the entire length of my shaft has me ready to lose it. I'm almost mindless over wanting to thrust all the way to the back of her throat. But, I manage to keep it in check and instead, brush my thumbs against her jaw, silently telling her we'll try it her way.

For a little while.

Those fiery green eyes of hers stay locked on me the

entire time as her lips close around my cock and that hot, sexy mouth of hers takes every inch of me in. Deep. Perfect suction. Perfect fucking rhythm.

The growing fever racing through my bloodstream is starting to overrule all rational sense, overriding my ability to keep from shooting my cum down her tight little throat already.

See, this right here is why she can't have control. I want to, *need to,* be the best damn sex of her life. Past, present, and future.

Especially her future.

Because I'm that guy. The one who thinks about the future. I have to be that guy. I've got a kid at home, tens of dozens of investors around the world, thousands of employees all across the country, and millions affected by the decisions I make. They're all counting on me to have my shit together every second of every day. I'm connected to all of their futures.

But this is the first time in a really long while that *my* future feels connected to anyone but Hannah's.

It's damn unnerving.

All too soon, the pleasure is too fucking good and my brain is shutting down to the point where I almost take over then.

Almost.

She pulls back before I can though.

"Why'd you stop?" I ask hoarsely.

The determined expression she's wearing tells me I'm not going to like what she does next.

She says simply, "It has to be a give and take with us, Logan. You can't control everything all the time." And with that, she sits back on her heels.

She wouldn't.

The look in her eyes tells me she *would.* "Let me know when you're ready to have us on an even playing field."

She stands up then and actually does it.

She actually walks her sweet, feisty ass out of the storage room.

13

| NICOLE |

I can't believe I just did that.

I don't even have time to process what the fallout will be for riling the beast like that because I'm too busy trying to figure out where exactly I'm going to find a priest to exorcise this insanely bold (and impressively badass) demoness that has somehow possessed my body.

Maybe Google will know.

Suddenly, Logan's hand flashes out and wraps around my wrist before I can so much as yelp.

An instant later, I'm back in the storage room, being held captive against the wall of his tall, muscular frame, and holy crap, there's a storm brewing in those turbulent topaz eyes of his.

I pushed him too far...but in a *good* way. I see it in his expression, feel it in his touch.

"You want to know why I want to maintain control, sweetheart? I'll show you."

A deep, rumbling sound rolls through his chest like thunder for a long, heated second before his lips finally come crashing down against mine.

This kiss is nothing like our first. It's…untamed. *Unyielding.*

It's like he's laying some sort of claim on me and flat-out refusing to take no for an answer.

When I have to pull back a bit to drag some oxygen into my lungs and slow my racing heart, he dips his head down to skim his lips along my throat.

With his mouth over my thrumming pulse, he murmurs in a tone so low I feel it against my skin, "I fucking love the taste of you."

I don't even realize he's holding my hands in his until I feel him lift them up high to the shelf above me.

"Hold on," he says as he slowly grazes his thumbs back and forth over my hardened nipples now straining through my taut t-shirt.

As he watches me fight back a moan, his gaze grows hotter, darker. As intense as I've ever seen it. The expression on his face is more than just hungry, it's primal, almost predatory.

"Do you have any idea how many times I've wanted to touch you like this over the years?" he rasps. "It'd be all I could do not to grab your ropes and drag you close so I could get my mouth on these hard little nipples." He exhales harshly. "It's why I keep the AC so damn cold in your favorite climbing zones."

My thoughts immediately scatter. Partly because of the gritty, unbelievably sweet confession. But mostly as a result of the sharp shock of sensation I feel when his teeth close tightly over my nipple. Hard enough to make me feel the sting through my t-shirt and bra.

With carefully measured tugs, he gently increases the pressure, slowly wringing the most intensely exquisite pleasure-pain out of me and gradually pushing to my limits.

Soon, he's stealing control of every one of my senses, until the heat of his mouth is the single point of focus for my entire body.

When my limbs eventually start to quake uncontrollably from the pleasure, instantly, my nipple is released from its erotic vise, causing a wave of dizziness to overtake me.

He catches me before I even register I'm falling. "I told you to hold on," he tsks and moves his mouth to my other nipple.

Oh god, if he puts me through that again, I'll come.

"Logan—"

His body jerks like he's been whipped. "Say my name like that again and I'll be fucking you right here, right now with anyone and everyone listening."

The breathless sound that escapes me makes my thoughts on that plan abundantly clear.

He spins me around.

"You drive me crazy, woman."

Says the insanely hot pot to the innocent kettle.

It's possible I whispered that thought out loud.

His arms snap shut like steel bands surrounding me. I can't move, wouldn't want to even if I could. Every tense flex of his torso is sending a tingling rush down my spine, and the entire length of his stiff shaft is now rock hard against me.

"See how hard you made me with your little stunt earlier?" he growls softly, gently scoring his teeth over the back of my neck. "Best fucking head of my life. Until you stopped."

He slides one calloused hand up my ribcage to cup my breast while his other hand is down between my legs, pressing firmly over the seam of my jeans. Both are like hot, unmoving brands, their only apparent purpose to keep me tightly pinned to him.

And to torment me.

His lips move up to my ear. "Do you want me to touch you?"

I swear, nothing aside from climbing up a cliff has ever felt like this for me. The rush. The strain. The feeling of danger that makes the finish all the more worth it.

He's a climber, I know he feels it too. It's crackling in the air all around us. It's intense. *Exhilarating.*

Another grazing skim of his calloused thumb then, and a touch more pressure between my legs.

I can't even form any words to respond to his question. He's effectively scrambled my brain, overloaded my senses. All I can do is arch my back and rub my backside against the steel rod of his cock through his jeans.

"That's not an answer," he says gruffly.

Dammit. He's going to make me beg.

"Do you," he nips at my jawline, "want me to touch you?" He punctuates his question by slowly grinding his palm over my mound.

"Yes." The word echoes in my brain like a deafening shout, even though it comes out barely louder than a whisper.

"I didn't hear you," he murmurs, turning me back around to face him so he can gaze down at me and see every last expression on my face. "Say it again," he says, his hands now simply stroking my hair, no longer even in contact with my body.

"Please," I exhale instead, my cheeks blazing hot, while the rest of me feels cold without his touch.

Is this how I made him feel? Powerless. Aching. Almost desperate.

If it is, hell, it won't be the last time I do it to him, that's for damn sure.

It's like he can read my thoughts. He smiles. "Feisty." His mouth is back on my neck, his teeth scraping the sensitive skin there with just the right roughness.

"Please what?" he asks again, his breath hot against

my throat as he pulls me closer by the waistband of my jeans, the backs of his fingers teasing the top of my panties.

When I still refuse to answer, he chuckles and starts palming his erection with his free hand, nudging my now soaking wet slit with his knuckles. Even through two layers of fabric, I know he can feel it. The flare of his eyes tells me he knows exactly how wet he's made me.

Okay, he wins.

"Please, Logan. Please touch me."

A flash of triumph lights his expression before he grins and asks, "Where do you want me to touch you?"

Damn him. I know I deserve this payback but does he have to be so freaking good at it?

His tongue flicks over my collarbone. "Here?" he whispers.

I shake my head no. "My…" I can't say it.

"Your…?"

I realize then that my jeans are open. The air conditioning feels icy cold against my damp panties—an insane contrast to the heat coursing through me every time his skin simply touches mine.

"My pussy," I murmur finally, and his lips meet mine again as if to reward me for my confession.

He doesn't slide my jeans down like I expect though. Instead, he simply circles my clit with two fingers over my panties, with just enough pressure to keep me mindless with pleasure.

My legs feel like they're going to dump me on the floor. Thankfully, he backs me up without breaking contact until I feel the wall behind me to help keep me upright.

It's a wholly necessary precaution on his part, I discover, as he proceeds to dip his head down to close his teeth over my nipple. The other one, this time.

Meanwhile, his fingers begin a new pressure, a new pattern, seemingly custom-designed to drive me straight to the brink.

"I can't wait to suck on this hard little clit," he growls against my nipple.

My entire body instantly starts to tremble.

I feel the orgasm building, growing, tingling like charged static electricity sizzling through my veins and every inch of my body.

"Logan…" I gasp. "I'm going to…" My words splinter and my limbs start outright shaking, my vision very nearly whiting out.

He finishes the sentence for me, turning the single word into a raw, feral command.

"Come."

That's all it takes to send me over the edge.

Devastating waves of pleasure explode outward from my clit, making every nerve ending I possess feel simultaneously seized by a live current.

Even my attempts to drag oxygen into my lungs feel like licks of fire down my throat, but in the best possible way. My only comparison is when I'm nearly at the top of a mountain, my muscles screaming from the climb, the safety of the ground nowhere in sight, and the only air available to me almost punishingly thin.

That's when I realize every breath I'm exhaling is wrapped around his name.

I expect to find him triumphant over that fact, over the absolutely spectacular way he just paid me back for teasing him earlier. But his gaze is gentle, tender almost.

My fuzzy brain attempts to reboot enough to memorize that expression. The first—and only—time he's ever looked at me with that much naked affection.

But then he goes and splinters my thoughts again as he scrapes the stubble of his chin along the side of my neck and tells me roughly, "That was fucking beautiful."

Stepping back to button me up, he growls matter-of-factly, "You're going to do that for me again, sweetheart." He presses a hard, but gentle kiss against my lips. "But in my mouth, this time. Then on my fucking cock."

His stormy gaze pins me in place, harnessing me more effectively than any climbing ropes ever did. "But not until I say so."

Oh god. The man just got me off without even removing my jeans, and somehow, he has me halfway to another orgasm just from his words alone.

I'm in big trouble.

14

| NICOLE |

Ever since Logan got back from Vegas a few weeks ago, I feel like I've been in training for the *American Ninja Warrior* competition or something. Between climbing and all the other fantastically rigorous activities I've been doing with him, my body has never been this physically exhausted before.

I'm absolutely not complaining.

The fact that all said activities have yet to even get us past third base is downright impressive.

But, truth be told, it's the part *after* all the orgasms that I think I like best. There are times he'll just hold me, for minutes on end, like he doesn't want to let me go…and then he'll get all growly and demanding and *tell* me he doesn't want to let me go.

Though with a lot more colorful f-bombs, of course.

It's really terribly adorable. In a gruff bear-with-a-thorn-in-his-paw sort of way.

And I have to admit, every time, it gets harder to leave.

I'm getting in deep with the man, I know. Which is just crazy. This is *Logan* we're talking about here. There's a reason he's been single for the last nine years.

I've heard him tell his workers—on numerous occasions—that he purposely never dates any woman with the intention of starting a relationship. It's the same thing he tells reporters. He's very public about his stance on not looking to remarry. As he always says, his daughter is the only girl in his life now.

Period.

Where Logan's concerned, I believe it.

And to be honest, I can't blame him. If there were ever a woman to carry a torch over, Janine would be it. She was...perfect. So perfect that I can't even be envious of her for having the love of a man beyond her lifetime.

I actually kind of get it.

Because the more time I spend with Logan, the more I'm starting to think that maybe, perhaps, one day, in the far distant future...I might end up feeling the same way about him.

Which is again, just crazy.

"Nicole?"

I spin around and shine the flashlight on my keychain up, way up. "Kenny, what are you still doing here so late?" My evening clients are always scheduled a few hours before the gym closes because I usually spend those last couple of hours either climbing or watching the pros on the most advanced walls flabbergast the rest of us with their skills.

Kenny's session had ended nearly five hours ago.

He's been doing this more and more over the past two months. I've had a few chats with his psychologist and psychiatrist to see if they've also been noticing more erratic behavior from him and while they have, they weren't too overly concerned yet.

The difference for them, however, is that they're both men who aren't completely dwarfed by Kenny's linebacker-looking frame. I can't say the same for me.

I *am* starting to feel concerned. And frankly, more than a little uneasy around him.

"Heading home?" he asks as he taps his foot on the asphalt and fidgets around restlessly like he's agitated about something.

With the way he's opening and closing his fists, and the scowl that seems permanently affixed to his face, I'm definitely hearing alarm bells in my head.

"I'm actually meeting up with someone," I fib.

Logan and I *had* intended to go out and grab a bite and maybe a movie or something since Hannah's at a sleepover tonight, but he got called in to a late phone conference about an hour ago. At last text check, he was still at his corporate office in the city with no clear end in sight yet so he told me he'd bring takeout for a late dinner over to my place as soon as he could.

"I'm actually running late to meet him," I add, finding it surprisingly not at all difficult to lie to Kenny, which speaks volumes. If my gut instincts are telling me to get the heck out of there, I'm going to listen.

"*Him* being Logan?" sneers Kenny, with a bitter edge to his voice that has me adjusting my hold on my keys so they can be used as a self-defense weapon. "You're fucking him, aren't you?" His face twists into a snarl of disgust.

I don't respond. Instead, I swiftly take those last few steps over to my SUV. There are still quite a few cars in the lot so we're pretty well-hidden, unfortunately, and a good distance away from the front entrance. There isn't a single other person in the lot that I can see so my panic attack alarm won't do me any good. Locking myself in my car is definitely going to be the safest option here.

He snags a hand around my elbow. "Don't ignore me! You know how I hate that!"

I yank my arm free and pull open my door.

He slams it shut and shoves me up against it with one meaty paw, knocking my keys out of my hand as he gives me a hard shake that rattles my molars.

Waving a finger in my face, he snarls out, "I thought you were different."

With escape no longer an option, I begin locking and loading every psychological weapon at my disposal. "In what way, Kenny? How did you think I was different?"

Flat out fury is turning his expression frenzied, manic. "You weren't like all the others before. But now you are. Now that you're fucking Logan, you're going to end things with us, aren't you?"

According to Kenny's school records, he's been flying off the handle and getting into fights since he was young. Working with me through high school, he got to a place where he could keep his anxiety and rage under control. But then he started college and everything stable in his life disappeared. First his foster parents, then the few friends he had. Unfortunately, his abandonment issues have always been more his psychologist's domain.

It's clear those issues are huge triggers, but, since I haven't worked with him on these issues, all I can do is divert him away from those landmines until I have an opening to escape.

"What do you mean end things? You're one of my first clients. You've been with me the longest. Are you wanting to fire me?" I ask, turning the conversation on its side. "Have you been unhappy with our sessions?"

He frowns, confused over the tide change. "Our sessions are the only things that make me happy every week."

"Then I don't understand. Do you *want* to stop our sessions?" I feign supreme confusion.

"What? No!" He shakes his head violently, as if trying to clear it of his demons.

Yep, I'm mucking with his brain completely. His hand isn't pinning me against my car door anymore. If I can get him to back up a bit, I'll be home free.

"You're the one who's been too busy for me lately," he insists, his anger returning.

"The last couple of weeks, we've been meeting almost every other day," I counter. "I know your psychologist insists on meeting only once every two weeks. Is that what this is about? Is he wanting you to meet with me less? Do you need me to talk to him and explain?"

"I haven't told him," Kenny admits in a hushed tone.

I see a couple of folks leaving the gym out of the corner of my eye. If I can just keep Kenny talking a little longer, I may be able to signal for help.

Sure, this is a bit cliché—like getting the villain to talk too much until the cavalry arrives, but I'll take what I can get.

"Why haven't you told your psychologist about meeting with me? Do you think he'll disapprove?"

If I weren't frightened out of my mind right now, I'd be really freaking proud of this impressive psychological warfare I'm engaging in.

"He won't like me meeting with you so much. He always says I can't think of therapy as my only constant."

I couldn't have phrased it any better.

Frustrated tears gather in Kenny's eyes. "But he doesn't understand. I need you. I need you to be there for me. But you're abandoning me like all the others. None of you care about me."

He's starting to hit himself in the thigh and I know that time's almost up; he's getting ready to fly apart.

"You're going to leave me. Just like everyone else."

"I don't have to," I say, wording it just so.

"You're lying!"

I don't even see the back of his hand coming at me until I feel the pain exploding in my cheek.

I've never been struck before. And my brain is having a hard time recovering.

My eye is throbbing in its socket, but it's still functional enough to see he's getting ready to hit me again.

No way, asshole.

The next thing I know my limbs are attacking him like they have a mind of their own. I'm probably doing that chick-flailing-arm thing, but I don't care. His second punch doesn't land, that's all that matters.

I fight harder.

But, he's too big. Too strong.

Suddenly, he grabs me by the shoulders and slams me back onto the ground.

The explosion of pain knocks the wind out of me. My skull feels bashed in, and there's a throbbing, overwhelming pressure in my head now making my senses sluggish.

My vision's ebbing in and out, and my entire body feels injected with liquid lead. It's getting harder to move.

That's when I realize he's got his forearm on my throat, smothering my airway.

No.

I think I scream it. At least that's how it sounds to my ears.

His nose, his eyes, his crotch. Everything is fair game. I kick and slap and scratch and bite. I go downright ballistic on him.

Just don't stop fighting. You can't stop fighting.

15

| LOGAN |

Why the hell is Nicole still at the gym?

My gut's telling me something's wrong. I floor the gas pedal and tear through the parking lot, straight over to her SUV.

I'm still a few rows away when I see her.

She's on the ground between the cars and that Kenny kid is fucking attacking her.

I screech to a halt and get out of the car. I need to cut across the lot by foot. It'll get me there faster. At least I pray it will.

I've never run so fast in my life.

Never pushed past fear this paralyzing before.

There's no weapon that I can see, but goddammit, he's choking her. She's still defending herself like a wild cat though. And every fierce blow she continues to land gives me hope.

Nicole's a fighter. She'll hold on until I get there.

Please let me get to her in time.

What feels like an eternity later, I ram my entire body into his, my only goal to take him out like a wrecking ball. The guy's built like a tank, but I've got pure rage on my side.

I don't just tackle him, I body blow him clear into a nearby car, denting it. And hopefully him as well in the process.

Two men from the small crowd rush over to help jump in and restrain Kenny so I can run back to Nicole.

She's already getting up when I get to her. "I'm okay," she whispers jaggedly, her eyes struggling to focus as she grips the back of her head in pain.

"You're not okay. He was *choking* you, Nicole."

He could've killed her. The mere thought of that alone is enough to crush my heart in a punishing vise of pain so severe, getting it to keep pumping feels like a fucking miracle.

"Did he hit you? Are you in pain anywhere else?" I ask savagely, struggling—and failing—to hold my anger in check. It's literally taking every ounce of my control not to go back over to Kenny and beat him to a bloody pulp.

Nicole keeps one hand securely wrapped around my wrist. "Don't, Logan. I'm okay."

The cops get here minutes later to arrest Kenny and an ambulance for Nicole arrives seconds after.

A trip to the E.R. seems like a given to me, but she

keeps telling everyone she's fine.

"Really," she insists. "It's not that bad. I've been hurt worse on a climb. All I want are some ice packs and a couple of ibuprofen."

Clearly, she's in shock and not thinking right.

I'd already told Derick to get my on-site physician over here so he can do a full examination on her, and thankfully, he arrives at the tail end of Nicole's insane ice pack and ibuprofen suggestion.

"Oh no, not you again."

If I wasn't so worried about her right now, the fact that both doctor and patient just uttered that statement in stereo would've been pretty damn funny.

Right now, though, it's all I can do to keep my shit together.

I pace and hover, fully ready to get a portable whole-body MRI unit over here to scan her. When they don't ask for one, I welcome the chance for a third opinion from someone in the crowd who mentions he's a retired combat medic with two decades of trauma medicine experience.

The longest hour of my life later, they each give her the medical all-clear to go home.

I breathe again for what feels like the first time all night then I go over and yank her keys from her hand. "You're staying with me tonight."

"Logan, I'm fine. You heard the EMTs. *And* the military medic. *And* your board-certified physician. Kenny didn't manage to choke me for very long, and aside from a bruise on my cheek and a lump on the back of my head, I don't have a scratch on me."

I ignore the obviously head-traumatized crazy talk. "I've got five spare bedrooms, all full suites with their own bathrooms. Take your pick. Each is practically the size of your apartment."

I'm not exaggerating. Nicole's apartment is ridiculously small. The building security is shit. And most offensive of all, it's clear on the other fucking side of town.

"Logan, I can't stay with you."

"Why the hell not?"

"How would we possibly explain my spending the night to Hannah?"

"Easy. I'll tell her that since she got to have a sleepover, I had one, too."

A small, pained chuckle escapes her. "You're not funny."

"That's the head injury talking, sweetheart. We both know I'm hilarious." I carry her over to my car and buckle her up securely.

"We need to discuss this."

"As far as I'm concerned, the only thing we're discussing in your impaired mental state is if you want pancakes or waffles for breakfast. I'm okay waiting on you hand and foot for the first couple of days, but by next week, you'll need to start pulling your weight with the cooking."

She sighs. "You're being impossible."

Man, she really must have hit her head hard. I'm being a prince.

"What on earth are we going to tell Hannah?"

"Fine, we can tell her your house is being fumigated for some mutant bugs that will take time to get rid of."

"We can't *lie* to her."

"Then I'll make a call to get a real infestation going."

"Logan, be serious."

I settle into the car beside her. "I'm being dead serious. I don't want Hannah knowing you were attacked." It would traumatize her for sure. "So, this will be like a Santa Claus lie. You lie to kids about Santa Claus, right? No ethical objection to that?"

She scowls. "I don't like when you out-argue me."

"Feel free to blame your head injury and not my superior debating skills." I lean over to press a gentle kiss to her forehead. "Rest and recover for a couple weeks at my place. We can pick up this argument after that."

Then, to make absolutely certain this will go my way, I suppress all my natural tendencies and say, "I'm asking you here. For me. Will you please stay at my place until we know that Kenny's locked up for good and unable to hurt you again? For my own peace of mind?"

A soft smile transforms her tired expression. "Okay. If you're sure."

Why the whole me-asking-instead-of-demanding

thing can get her to agree to things is a mystery to me, but I'm grateful she's finally seeing reason. "Get some rest, sweetheart. I'm going to take us the long way home. Less bumps in the road."

She nods and starts to close her eyes.

When we're about halfway out of the parking lot, however, her eyes blink back open. "Hey, how did you know to come find me at the gym?"

"I tracked your GPS location on your phone tonight."

"Oh. I didn't even know my phone could do that."

"It can't. Not unless you have a hacker looking for you. Or you have the app I installed on your phone the other week…the same one I have on Hannah's phone."

"I see."

I expect her to be pissed that I lo-jacked her. Surprisingly, she's not. And I'm wholly curious as to why. "Aren't you going to yell at me?"

"No," she answers muzzily.

Is it totally screwed up that I'm a bit disappointed?

"I figure," she says as she slowly starts sliding into sleep, "with me staying at your place, I'll have plenty of opportunities."

"To argue with me?" Yeah, it's pretty fucked up how much that cheers me up.

"Nope." She smiles. "To get even."

Good lord, I'm crazy about this woman.

16

| NICOLE |

It's been over two weeks now since the attack and I'm still staying at Logan's.

I'm beginning to think I might be living here. Sort of. It's all very unclear.

Logan insists this lack of clarity on when exactly we're planning on me moving back to my apartment is all because I suffered an extensive brain trauma. And after giving me this medical diagnosis of his, he immediately finds a way to distract me and change the subject.

The man is positively incorrigible. And so very, very adorable.

He doesn't distract me with sex per se—he's pretty adamant about me needing more time to recover before we can argue about that topic. It's been more...creatively comprehensive foreplay, if you will.

Like I need any more reasons to want to stay longer.

The orgasm-on-demand amenities at Casa De Logan

are of course, great, but I've honestly loved every single minute of my time here. From the board game nights to the afternoons spent simply hanging out in the back yard, it's all been wonderful.

I know it can't last, but I'm cherishing each moment as it comes.

Today, we're grilling outside with Logan's parents. I've been looking forward to it all week. It's my first backyard barbecue ever, sad as that sounds. And seriously, I'm so excited I might need a tiny mood stabilizer.

"Hi Grandma!" Hannah rushes over to give Carol a hug. "Look! Look! Nicole is living with us now! Isn't that awesome?"

Oh my god. "It's just temporary," I tell her quickly. "We're not 'living together.'"

"Logan already explained everything, dear."

I shoot a surprised glance over at Logan.

He shrugs. "I'm convinced my mother has some kind of super invasive surveillance on my life. I've thought so since I was a kid."

"Gee, I wonder what that's like," I deadpan.

"Rhetorical humor is lost on me," he informs me, tickling my ribs mercilessly for a second for attempting to liken his actions to his mother's. "Anyway, she's basically psychic when it comes to my life and always seems to knows everything. So, I don't bother trying to keep things from her anymore."

Carol nods matter-of-factly. "This is true. And we're in absolute agreement that you shouldn't go back to your apartment. Those bugs Logan described sound absolutely dreadful."

I raise an eyebrow at Logan.

Who's gone missing into the other room.

"Luckily," I say, not at all comfortable 'Santa Claus lying' to his parents. "The fumigation should be done soon." I don't want her to think my home is a biohazard zone.

"I heard it's going to take longer," he calls out, still eavesdropping out of sight.

As Carol sets the picnic place settings outside, she weighs in, "Best not to rush these things. You can't be too careful with insect infestations."

"Oh yay!" cheers Hannah from the lawn where she's throwing horseshoes with Phil. "Does that mean Nicole can stay with us longer? I love having her here. She's so much fun!"

Gah, that little girl knows just how to melt my heart.

"Hold up," says Logan, materializing out of nowhere. "Are you saying Nicole is more fun than your old man?"

Hannah ponders this question seriously for a bit. "Okay, maybe not more fun," she says diplomatically. "But she is more fun*ny*. Especially when she's driving you crazy."

"She does do that often," agrees Logan.

"Only because your father starts it," I counter.

"I know!" says Hannah, cracking up. "It's *so* much fun to watch. It's like watching grandma and grandpa pretend to fight."

Carol pats Phil lovingly on the shoulder. "Oh, we're not pretending, dear. Your grandfather drives me bonkers."

"But you still kiss and make up after," Hannah reasons. "That's what makes it more like pretend fighting. Just like what Dad and Nicole do."

I don't know that she fully understands what she just implied, but I'm fairly certain all the adults are thinking the same thing.

Phil tosses a very interested gaze over at Logan, who is hyper-focused on the grill at the moment.

Meanwhile, I'm avoiding Carol's eyes altogether. I have a feeling Logan might be right about her being partially psychic.

As a therapist, this intrigues me. As a woman in an undefined live-in relationship with her son, I'm quaking in my sneakers.

I quickly re-route the discussion to the food Phil placed on the table earlier. "These dishes you all brought look amazing." That a lot of them appear to be meat-free makes me all gooey inside.

Carol beams. "They're all vegetarian. I've been trying out recipes all week."

"She has," says Phil. "And when all those turned out really badly, we had our special events chef whip up some things for us to bring this morning."

Carol blushes and gives her husband a killing look. "Narc."

Lordy, these two. "You really didn't have to go to any trouble just for me."

"Nonsense." Carol gives my hand a motherly squeeze. "It's good for us to try new things and eat healthier. Logan's been trying to get us to cut out red meat for years."

"I still don't know how he does that," I say. "Steaks and burgers are way too good for me to give up forever."

"Wait, so you're *not* a vegetarian?" asks Phil, confused.

"Nicole's only a vegetarian six days a week," clarifies Logan. "On Sundays, all bets are off. I'm not even exaggerating; the woman is like a carnivorous dinosaur. Hell, she'll bite your hand off if you try and take her meat away from her."

"Or if you bad-mouth about her football team," adds Hannah, giggling.

"Got the teeth marks to prove it," says Logan, eyes silently daring me to contradict him.

I can't believe they're ganging up on me like this. The first incident Hannah saw was just a joke, and the second, Logan is presenting totally out of context. Not that I can possibly put it into context for his parents. Seeing as how I'd bitten him on his rump and all.

"Logan dear, why don't you try this six-day thing?" suggests Carol brightly. "That way, on Sundays, when we grill over at our house, I won't have to make one sad little pasty turkey burger to get shamed on the grill by all the others."

"OMG," laughs Hannah. "Nicole makes fun of Dad's burgers, too."

Again, out of context. I didn't make *fun* of them, I simply mentioned them while Hannah was reading *Bunnicula*, the classic tale of the vampire rabbit who sucks vegetables pale. Sheesh.

"Hey Dad," inquires Hannah curiously. "If you start eating red meat again, does that mean we can start eating fast food burgers?"

Uh oh.

Logan gives me a see-what-you-started look, which then transforms into a grin much too quickly for my comfort.

I brace myself for whatever he has in store.

"Tell you what, Nicole," he offers genially. "Let's make a deal. I'll let you grill me a steak on Sundays from now on *if* you let me do your laundry at the same time."

I gasp, scandalized that he could even suggest such a thing.

"Nicole here believes whole-heartedly in sports superstitions," he fills his parents in, chuckling at my attempt to vaporize him on the spot with my eyes. "She thinks if she does her laundry on Sundays, her precious 49ers will lose."

"Why test fate? Every time I've done laundry on NFL Sundays, they've lost," I defend, before smacking him on the shoulder. "Stop trying to make me look crazy in front of your parents."

"Wasn't trying to," he says, before smiling evilly. "If I *really* wanted to do that, I'd have told them how you buy extra underwear every fall to make sure you have enough clean pairs available since you also don't do laundry on NFL Mondays and NFL Thursdays whenever San Fran has a winning streak…rare as that may be."

I can see his parents are trying not to laugh.

And I start surveying the utensils to see which one will do the most non-vital damage if I throw it at Logan.

"I think that kind of fan devotion is to be commended," says a straight-faced Carol, ever the gracious one.

"It really is," agrees Phil with a reassuring smile. "In fact, I'd probably have done something like that when I was your age."

I give Logan a smug 'so there' look.

"Really, Grandpa?"

"Sure," he says. "You know, if my team stunk as badly as the 49ers."

My jaw drops.

"Nicole dear, you really should change your

allegiance to the Broncos," says Carol with a grave nod like she's sad to be the bearer of bad news. "That way, you could take Logan up on his deal. Win-win."

Unbelievable.

The resulting 'so-there' look from Logan is infinitely smugger than mine.

Good god, downright atrocious sports taste aside, I just can't get enough of this family.

17

| NICOLE |

"Just out of curiosity, are we *ever* going to have sex?"

Logan pauses what he's doing and shoots me a look that's more curious than surprised by my question. "You don't consider what we've been doing sex?"

A couple of things I've learned about Logan over the time I've gotten to know him. He hardly gets caught off-guard. And he appreciates bluntness. Prefers it, really.

"Before the Kenny thing, you told me you were going to make me come on your cock," I say, fighting back a blush. "And you haven't yet."

Can't get any more blunt than that.

"Because you had a really traumatic thing happen to you, baby."

"And I've sat down with a colleague who specializes in post-trauma assessment just to be doubly sure I'm all good. Because I *knew* you'd demand a second opinion."

"Who was the first?" he asks, unconvinced. "Anyone

I know?"

I sigh. "Me, Logan."

"Oh." He looks like he wants to argue.

But he also looks like he's fighting a massive hard-on.

As much as I do enjoy doing the first with him, the second is much more interesting to me at the moment.

"I love when you make me come, Logan, I do. But...I want more. I want to feel you come in my mouth for once. And I really, really want to feel you inside of me."

"*Jesus Fucking Christ.* You're not playing fair."

When the stakes are sex with the most handsome, sweet, maddening man I know?

Nope, zero fairness required.

"I'm ready, Logan. I swear. I want this."

"Hell, I do, too." He stalks me to the bed and grabs his shirt to wrench it off. "Are you sure, baby? Because once I have you, I'm never going to want to stop," he warns, his low, growling voice making that the sexiest threat I've ever heard in my life.

Instantly, I feel my panties become drenched. "Yes. God, yes."

His lips crash into mine a second later, rewarding me for my answer with a deep, primal, soul-reaching kiss that steals every last thought from my brain.

Before I know how it even happens, I'm naked.

And so is he.

I'll never get over the sight of his body. Miles of tightly corded muscle, tense, tight, and powerful. Tall, but the perfect height to cradle me.

He pulls me flush against him and places a gentle kiss on my shoulder, nipping at my flesh tenderly as he says, "If you want me to stop at any time, you just say the word, okay?"

I nod my head, unable to speak with his naked body finally pressing against mine.

Then his next kiss hits me like a gale force wind. Raw, unbridled. All take and no give.

My knees buckle.

"I've got you. I won't let you fall," he murmurs in my ear before his lips touch the sensitive skin along my neck.

I shiver as the memory of him saying those very words to me five years ago hit me. I'd replayed the moment countless times over the years. He'd been climbing beside me, giving me pointers on the wall, and I'd slipped. He immediately swung over to cloak me with his body until I could find my bearings again.

"You said that to me the first time you started talking to me again."

"I remember," he says hoarsely. "And I remember feeling this same craving for you, even back then. Having you in my arms that day was the beginning of the end for me, I think."

His words wrap themselves around my heart just as

securely as his arms wrap around my body as he lifts me up onto the bed. Then I'm airborne for the briefest of seconds as he drops me onto the center of his giant king-size mattress before he covers what feels like every inch of me with his body fully for the first time ever.

The sensation is almost overwhelming. With every hot touch of his skin against mine, everything in me hums to life then as if my body has been waiting for this very moment to wake up.

I wonder if it'll always be like this with him, if he'll always manage to make me feel both safe and profoundly out of control all at once.

"You set the pace for this first time, baby," he says, sitting back and pulling me up onto his lap. "I don't want to hurt you."

I run my fingers through his hair as I straddle him, loving the feel of my breasts crushing to his chest, the flesh of my butt tightly clenched in his hands.

"I want to make this last, sweetheart, so you're going to have to work with me here." His voice is taut, tight.

I tilt my head back to meet his gaze.

"You're rubbing your sweet little clit against the head of my cock," he grits out.

Oh. I hadn't even realized I'd been rocking against him. Judging by how wet I am, that makes sense.

He captures my lips with his before I can apologize. "Forget I said that. Anything you want. However you want it."

God, this man. I can see the strain, the struggle for him to give me total control.

I feel his hand slip between us so he can grip the base of his cock and hold it steady for me.

When on earth did he manage to put on a condom?

He chuckles. "Your brain talks a lot when you're in the moment." He brushes his lips against mine with affection. "I like it."

I rise up onto my knees and nudge myself against the broad head of his cock.

The next thing I know, my concentration splinters at the feel of his hot mouth sucking on my nipple.

A gasping moan shudders out of me.

"Sorry," he says, not sounding all that apologetic. "But you can't flaunt your perfect breasts in my face and not expect me to want a taste."

Incorrigible. "Don't stop," I tell him as I position his long, hard shaft at my slick entrance and slowly sink down onto him, one impossibly thick inch at a time.

"Jesus, you're fucking tight," he rumbles, the corded muscles of his neck straining with tension and his labored breathing sounding like he's barely holding on.

He's not even halfway inside of me when I start to feel implausibly stretched, filled to my limit. Oh lord, he's far too big; he'll never fit.

"Yes, I will."

Wow, I really do think out loud during sex.

The deeper I try to take him, the more I question if I even can. I'm in a state of suspended shock, I think, need coursing through my veins like molten fire even as my brain keeps telling me that this is physically just not possible. "Help me, Logan."

His entire body stills. "Do you want to stop?"

"*No.* I need you to take over. Please. I need you to—"

The air whooshes out of my lungs as my back hits the mattress.

But instead of fucking me right then and there, Logan stares down at me for a beat, slowly running his calloused hands up my torso, spanning my ribs and leaving a trail of heat in their wake.

"So damn beautiful." His eyes lock onto mine as he reaches down to fist his thick shaft and slowly circle the broad tip around my clit, each hot, hard glide devastatingly intense, the pleasure almost unbearable.

I feel my legs start shaking, and my heartbeat racing out of control, the former because he's playing my body like his own personal instrument, but the latter is because of the way he's looking at me the entire time.

Eyes half-mast with hunger, jaw grit with tension, he pushes his wide cock into me gradually, inch by inch, until by some miracle, he's buried to the hilt.

"Told you I'd fit, baby." He brushes his lips against

mine. "You were fucking made for me." With that gritty decree, he pulls back and plunges inside me in one long, hard thrust. So deep I see starbursts of color shooting across my vision.

"Tight, hot little pussy designed just for my cock," he rasps in my ear, pure, primal possession throbbing in his voice with each word.

He sits me back on top of him, gripping me by the waist as he slowly drives his cock up into me from base to tip and back, at a fluid, measured pace that has me feeling every single inch of him, hot and thick inside me.

It's almost too much, too perfect, his gruff hands locked on my hips, the granite-like muscles of his chest rubbing against my nipples with every thrust.

"Ready to come for me, sweetheart?"

In reply, I sink my teeth down on the strong, taut tendons of his neck.

Growling, he lifts me up and starts fucking me on his cock. Hard and fast. Rough and relentless.

I swear, sometimes he makes me feel so tiny. The intensely sexy way he's pounding me up and down on his shaft like I don't weigh a thing, literally all I'm able to do is hold on for the ride as he races me toward an orgasm that I already know is going to destroy me.

His lips capture mine just as everything around me implodes in a blizzard of blinding white.

I'm lost in a freefall, a thousand feet off a mountain

with no ground in sight, until his hands clamp down to hold me tight against him.

"I've got you," he murmurs roughly as hot shards of pleasure begin exploding outward from my core.

The world shifts once more and he's on top of me, cradling me gently, holding me tightly until I can safely return back to earth.

"Fuck, I love when you come." He lifts his head to look down at me in lust-filled adoration.

Then he gives me exactly three more seconds to recover before he presses a gentle kiss to my lips and says hoarsely, "My turn, now."

| LOGAN |

I flip her over gently.

Well, as gently as I can, given the fact that I'd been seconds from coming half a dozen times while she'd been bouncing on my cock.

"Drop your head down onto the pillow, baby," I order, my voice a rough, ragged whisper as I try to calm the hell down.

Shyly, she does just that, lifting her sweetly rounded ass up to me. And fuck, the sight of that alone is making it hard not to blow my load right then and there.

From that first climb on the wall when I'd had her body cradled back against me, I'd wanted to take her like this.

Now, with the dream so close to reality, I'm fighting not to explode on contact.

I give myself a few more seconds to get my lust in check before I squeeze one sexy little ass cheek in each hand and spread her wide, driving my cock into her in one hot, slick thrust.

So damn perfect.

The sheet crumples in her fists as she moans out my name. No way in hell I can stop or even slow down now, not with her pushing back against me, her wet slit drenching my shaft as she meets me stroke for stroke.

I watch as my cock plunges in and out of her, each time deeper, harder than the last, as I pound out my need inside of her.

I'm not going to last much longer.

Stretching her body back down on the mattress, I kiss my way up her spine and crush her to my chest, still buried deep in her tight pussy as I wrap my arms around her. With one hand pinching her nipple, I slide the other one down to rub her hot little clit.

I already know that this is going to be fucking mind-blowing for me, but I want it to be that way for her. Every time.

"L-Logan," she pants. "I'm going to come too fast if you keep doing that. I don't want to pass out before I feel you come inside me."

At her whispered confession, I stop. Christ, the woman is so damn sweet.

"Turn over, baby. I need to see your face when you come. When I come."

Instead of rolling fully onto her back, she turns onto

her side and hooks one leg over mine so I'm scissored against her, with the soft silky inner thigh of her other leg brushing against my balls.

"Like this?" she asks, eyes locked onto mine.

Then she goes and squeezes her pussy gently around the head of my cock.

Dammit all to hell, I just lose it and plow my entire throbbing shaft all the way back into her in one hard plunge, deeper than even I thought I could go.

"*Fuck.* Did I hurt you?" I manage to grit out as I sit back up while keeping her flush against me, not wanting to give up the position that's making me feel every single pulse of her pussy gripping my dick like a tight vise.

"N-no," she gasps. "More, Logan. Just like that. Hard. Deep."

Jesus Christ. "You're going to fucking ruin me," I tell her before driving into her again and again. I begin an almost brutal, unforgiving pace then, plowing into her with so much pent-up lust, I feel my brain beginning to separate from my body.

Suddenly, her pussy tightens around me from tip to base. She's coming hard on my cock, even harder than the last time, and a river of wetness is sliding me in even *deeper*, until I can't fucking hold back anymore.

Pleasure unlike anything I've ever experienced surges through my veins as I thrust one last time, shooting my cum hot and deep inside her.

I don't stop fucking coming until I'm seconds away from blacking out.

Eventually, with every last drop of cum wrung out of me and every last muscle in my body basically wrecked and useless, I collapse beside her and spoon her sweet, sexy little body against mine.

Tucking her in close, the perfect fit of her in my arms is the last thing I register before the world disappears into darkness.

* * * * *

She's still asleep.

After nearly a decade of not having a woman stay in my bed till morning, I thought this all would take some adjusting. But seeing Nicole in my bed just feels *right.*

I decide I want to do one of those perfect guy things and make her breakfast in bed so I give her a quick kiss, make sure she's nice and warm, and then head down to get cooking.

With the pancakes on the griddle I call Hannah over at her nana's house to chat. While I love it that Janine's parents take her sailing whenever she goes over to visit them, I worry about her every time she goes out on the water. So, I always make sure to get a full rundown of their plans before they head out.

I'm just hanging up the phone and flipping the last

pancake when I hear a ruckus upstairs.

I'm not worried.

Whistling to myself, I pour two mugs of coffee and set it on the tray with the food right about when the yelling starts.

"It burns! It burns!"

I chuckle.

"How *could* you, Logan?!"

The hysterical woman sounds like she's stopped, dropped, and rolled on the floor.

Honestly, she can be so entertaining at times.

I walk into the bedroom to see her naked on the bed giving the evil eye to the Broncos shirt I'd slipped her into while she slept. It's now balled up on the ground clear on the other side of the room, and I actually think she's trying to make it spontaneously combust by her glaring alone.

Somehow, I knew she wouldn't keep it on for very long.

Good thing I'd taken a photo of her in it before starting breakfast.

"Get me some holy water!" she demands.

Laughing, I go over to give her a kiss. "How about breakfast instead?"

Her eyes widen and soften when she sees the spread I made for us. "I've never had breakfast in bed before."

"So, it's a morning of firsts, then. Breakfast in bed, and you wearing the right team's apparel for a change." I can't help it, I'm still laughing. She's so fucking adorable.

"You laugh now, but I'm going to get you back." She arches up to give me a kiss before making room on the bed next to her.

"I don't think one of your tiny little 49ers t-shirts are going to fit me, babe."

Calm now, she sips at her coffee and gives me an evil smile. "If you think my t-shirts are tiny, wait until you wake up in one of my 49ers panties."

Mental note: Sleep with one eye open from now on.

Still totally worth it.

19

| LOGAN |

With the last of my Saturday meetings done, I head over to the gym to try and get a climb in with Nicole before dinner.

It's become our thing. Some couples go out on dates, we go up different walls together.

I fucking love it. Not just the climbing, but also how adamant the pushy little thing gets about me climbing at least once a week to offset my workaholic tendencies.

I've never really had someone look out for me like this before. To the point of adorably vicious verbal threats that usually have me laughing so hard, I can't focus on work anyway.

The woman really has been a breath of fresh air in my life. And in Hannah's.

Truthfully, the way she barged into our lives did take some getting used to. It wasn't easy for me to accept that I couldn't help Hannah as much I wanted to after the bullying. Being the one to make it all better used to be my specialty. And as much as it gutted me to have to stand on the sidelines for the first time in my kid's life, I'm grateful for Nicole.

I've definitely seen a positive difference in Hannah throughout all this. She isn't just happier and more talkative in public, she's bolder, surer of herself. More outgoing and expressive, but also more grounded, seems like.

And according to my mother, Nicole has been having the same effect on my being happier and more grounded as well.

As I walk into the gym and make my way upstairs, I hear the sound of her laughter nearby, and immediately, I feel myself smiling…and fighting off an instant hard-on.

It's an auto-response that I'm beginning to think may be a permanent one.

I follow the sound over to my office, where I find Derick (dammit) hamming it up for her in the hall outside *our* storage room. Mine and Nicole's.

Seriously, there are times I really want to fire the guy.

Yes, I'm intensely possessive of everything related to my relationship with Nicole. But this right here is more than that. The persistent dick has been hitting on her for years, ever since she started coming in here regularly. It's always annoyed me, but now, it pisses me the hell off.

She's *mine*.

Time to nip this shit in the bud.

I wrap an arm around Nicole and kiss her square on the mouth. Much to Derick's utter shock. Never really considered myself a man who likes public displays of affection before, but with Nicole, hell, I want the whole fucking world to see.

He holds up his hands in defeat. Message received.

In theory, I know I could just stop here. But we're talking *years* of him hitting on her.

After pressing a soft kiss against her temple, I draw back and casually say, "Hey, did you know that Derick here is the biggest Raiders fan I know?"

She gasps and stares at him as if he's the devil incarnate. "You like the *Raiders?*"

Derick lights up. "You watch football? Who's your team?"

"The 49ers of course."

He barks out a laugh. "They suck. I don't know why everyone tries to make this whole big rivalry between Oakland and San Fran. There's no competition. The 49ers are weak. Lucky at best."

Oh, shit.

"You take that back," she growls.

He laughs again. "No way. They're the worst team in the league if you ask me."

Great, now I have a ticking time bomb in my arms. I carefully pick up the now nuclear reactive woman and place her gently on the couch, fuming and *seething* mad.

Dammit, Derick had to go and ruin my fun. I just wanted him to stop hitting on the woman, not get potentially coldcocked by her. "You should probably go before she goes postal on you."

That's when he finally notices Nicole's giving him a death glower from the couch.

"Ah," he says, nodding in understanding. "Well played."

"Thanks."

Peering at her over my shoulder, he asks then, "Does she have any strong feelings toward any NBA teams? Because football season *is* almost over—"

I shove him out of my office and lock the door.

When I turn back, I see she isn't all that pleased with me either. "Was that absolutely necessary?"

I try to—but fail—at smothering my grin. "I really didn't think it would be quite so effective. I kind of forgot how much he likes trash talking other teams."

"Not the football thing." She frowns. "The part where you kissed me to mark your territory. I didn't like it."

"First of all, I kissed you because it's been half a day since I've had your lips on mine and I missed the hell out of you. Second of all, I wasn't marking my territory. I just wanted him to know that he couldn't hit on you anymore."

"How is that different?"

"Because it's you who fucking owns me, woman. I don't want anyone else. You're all I think about, all I want.

That's what I was showing him back there."

A reluctant smile tips her lips up at the corner. "Now who's not playing fair?"

"I'm not playing, period. I'm yours. In every sense of the word. But, it's okay if you don't want to tell me you feel the same."

"It is?"

"Yes."

"I see. And why is that, exactly?"

She's so damn cute when she uses her therapist voice and 'redirect questions' on me. "Because I already know you're mine. If you're not ready to say it out loud yet, it's okay. I can wait. In the meantime, I'll just have to make sure I ruin you for all other men until you're ready to admit it."

I yank her legs out from under her and have my mouth on her slick, sweet pussy the instant her back hits the couch cushion. "So, you take your time thinking about this. And only tell me yes when you really, truly feel it."

She practically screams when I start flicking my tongue across her clit.

"You're cheating," she pants when I ease back and finally give her a chance to breathe.

"Yes, I am." I slide two fingers along her g-spot while grazing my lips over her soft belly, up to her perfect little tits.

"What about now?" My teeth gently score over one tight, berry-hard nipple as I start to pump my fingers deep inside of her. "Are you feeling a little like mine now?"

Instead of answer, she stretches out fully on the couch and reaches her hand out to grab my hard cock.

Fuck, I love how this woman argues.

I groan as she quickly undoes my zipper and runs her tongue up the shaft, sucking at the tip when I start leaking precum like crazy.

Just when I start thrusting into her hot, wet mouth, the realization of where we are crashes over me.

Jesus Christ, I need to get some window blinds in this damn office.

As much as I want nothing more than to sixty-nine the hell out of her right now, we can't. Yes, the only folks who could possibly see us on the couch would have to be up high on one of the advanced walls across the gym peering with binoculars into my office window. But still, it's not worth the risk.

"Nicole, we can't do this here. It's too dangerous. I won't be able to keep myself in check. If you put that sexy mouth of yours on my cock again, the next thing you know, I'll be buried balls deep inside of you, fucking you until we both pass out."

She lets out a quiet, muffled moan, her wet pussy drenching the palm of my hand.

Fucking hell.

"You make me crazy," I murmur roughly before repositioning us so my back is to the window, blocking any possible view of her as I drop down between her thighs to run my tongue over her sugary slit. Spreading her wide, I form a seal over her hot little pussy with my lips as I begin tracing an array of alphabets over her pulsing flesh with my tongue...in *multiple* languages.

"Logan, don't stop..." she whimpers, her throat hoarse.

I growl at the insane and downright *unacceptable* idea of stopping right now and her whole body stiffens at the vibration.

Ruthlessly, I hold her on that brink just like that until finally, I hear my name slip past her lips in little moans of pure pleasure. "Logan, Logan, Logan," each a half a heartbeat apart, in a rhythm I could set a clock by.

Suddenly, her entire body snaps taut and her cries grow louder, harder, faster.

I capture her lips with mine before I let her plunge over that edge.

A long while later, after she's dozed off for a mini-nap, she lifts her head up from my chest and whispers, "I do...really, truly feel the same about you." She cuddles deeper into my arms. "And yes, I kind of want everyone to know it, too."

Ah, damn. Knowing it and hearing her tell me are two completely different things.

"That seals your fate, woman."

20

| NICOLE |

"You've got this! You're doing awesome," I call up to Hannah as she makes it up her tallest climb yet.

Lordy, I've missed hanging out with her every day.

Though Logan wasn't at all happy about it, I moved back into my apartment about a week and a half ago after we got word that Kenny was admitted to an institution.

Without that looming factor—and no actual insects in my apartment—there really wasn't a plausible reason we could give Hannah for me continuing to live there.

The bottom line was that I didn't want to keep lying to Hannah and his parents. And I didn't want to keep pretending my time there was more than what it was.

Though it had felt more right than anything in my life to this point, we'd essentially been playing house that entire time…with Santa Claus as our cover, a history we still haven't truly unburied, a traumatic event as the impetus of it all, and deepening feelings we still couldn't voice yet.

Our living together with that many psychological red flags just wasn't healthy.

Logan had wanted me to stay, I know. But, he didn't stop me. Not after I told him that I'm willing to wait however long it takes until those red flags are all addressed, until it's all real for us, and no longer pretend.

A lifetime, even.

"Yes!" cries out Hannah from the top of the wall.

I smile up at her. "Way to go, Hannah!"

Waving excitedly, she shoots me an elated grin and starts rappelling down like a pro. I watch and wait for her, anticipating the moment she touches down. It's easily the best part of my day on most days.

True to form, the second her feet hit the floor, she does a triumphant fist punch high into the air like a rockstar with a mic, before doing something akin to a touchdown end zone dance that ends with her hi-fiving anyone who wants to hi-five her.

I could watch that every day.

"Again!" she says, running over after she finishes her celebration dance. Her face is red from exertion, but she looks pumped, on top of the world.

"You sure you don't want to tackle a different climb instead?" I ask, not because I doubt her ability to handle it, but simply as a reminder for her to be mindful of her body and her limits. "This one was pretty tough."

"I liked it. And there's a different route I want to try,"

she says with a confidence she simply never had before. It's just amazing to see it blossom like this.

"Not too tired?" I press.

"Nope, I'm good." She turns to face the wall and I step back to watch as she finds her handholds.

In no time at all, she's hoisting her body up a more difficult route than she tried the last time, all of her movements bold and impressively well-chosen.

"Slow down a bit," I call up when I see a telltale wobble in her limbs. "Take a breather if you need to."

That's when I feel the back of my neck prickle. I glance over my shoulder and see that Logan's watching us from his office. He doesn't look happy at all, but, he stays where he is.

"Nicole!"

I shoot my gaze back over to Hannah and see she's lost a handhold.

"Don't panic. Find your grip," I call out, trying to talk her through her fears, while trying not to show any of mine.

Her body's clearly too tired. I should've told her not to go up again.

"I can't reach!" Hannah cries out, dread filling her voice.

For an adult, it wouldn't have been as big a problem, but being that she's a child—and a petite one at that—the nearest handhold would take a lot out of her to get to.

She's officially starting to panic. Now, every quick

glance she casts at the ground looks seized with terror.

"Deep breaths, Hannah. Look at the wall and remember you can do this." I see her shaking, struggling to hold on as her loose hand scrambles to find a secure grip.

Two of Logan's workers immediately begin rappelling to get to her. They're way at the top though; they won't make it in time.

C'mon Hannah. You can do this.

Finally, she makes a desperate lunge for a nearby foothold. But, her grip simply isn't strong enough to make it work.

With a shriek, she falls.

It's a nearly thirty-foot drop. The fact that she's on a part of the wall with no jagged formations jutting out for her to slam into is a small comfort. But still, with spine injuries being known to happen from those heights for grown men twice her size, seeing her tiny frame go down is nothing short of terrifying.

The harness catches her cleanly, and aside from a sharp jerk of her entire body that gives me a mini heart attack, she looks uninjured. At least physically.

With tears streaking down her face, and terrified hiccups racking her tiny frame, Hannah runs right past me to Logan, who catches her in his arms.

He's furious.

I can see it in the hard line of his lips, the stone set of his features.

"You okay?" he asks her, but she doesn't answer.

He glares at me, positively *enraged.*

Gently rocking her back and forth, he simply holds her until she stops crying.

I don't leave their side, even though I think Logan kind of wishes I would.

"You did a great job up there, Hannah," I say. "You fought through your fear, we all saw it. You pushed past it and reached for that last foothold to stabilize—we all would've tried the same thing. You didn't let your fear stop you."

"But I still fell," she mumbles dejectedly.

"Everyone falls. The important thing is that you didn't let your fear get the best of you. And that you don't let your fear stop you from trying again."

Logan snaps. "Are you out of your damn mind?"

"We'll wait until her muscles have had time to rest a bit, but when she's up for it, she needs to try again. Even if it's just part way up. She needs to know she can do this."

"Stop telling me what *my* kid needs to do," he growls, sounding beyond pissed. "She needs to be safe. Something that *you* failed to ensure when you let her go up that last climb even though her body was obviously fatigued."

"Logan."

"She's done." Without another word, he unhooks her harness. Judging by the look in his eyes, I can tell he isn't just referring to her being done with climbing today.

Hannah holds onto her harness. "I want to go again."

"If she wants to go again, you need to trust her."

"Just stop it!" he all but bellows at me. "This is my daughter's safety you're putting at risk just to prove that your methods aren't dangerous and reckless."

| NICOLE |

I recoil, cut to the bone by his assessment of the situation.

But I don't back down. "Logan, as I told you months ago, I'm not reckless. Every decision I make is in my clients' best interests."

"Is that how you see Hannah? As just one your clients?"

No. No, I don't. But that's a different discussion altogether. "It's important that she take these calculated risks."

"Operative word being 'risk.' She's too young to make decisions involving risk, and clearly, you're not the right person to be making any such decisions for her either. She is *not* going up again." Logan sounds as angry as I've ever heard him.

Hannah looks devastated. "But Daddy, it's not her fault. And I really do *want* to—"

"I said no."

Tears flooding her eyes, Hannah stares up at him for a beat in utter disbelief, before she turns and rushes off the floor to the women's restroom.

Logan follows her, looking equally devastated. And ready to break down the door.

"You're not listening to her," I say quietly, as gently as I can.

He ignores me and makes his way to his office.

I slip in before he can shut me out. "Logan—"

"Look, I get that your intentions are good, but you're not a parent, so you don't know anything about having to say no to your child. Do you think this is easy for me?"

He's not yelling. And that makes the words hit me harder than a shout would have.

"With all due respect, Nicole, you don't get to tell me how to feel or how to decide what's best for my kid. You've never had to make the tough decisions a parent does. You've never had to wonder if this time, she's sick enough to go to the E.R. or if the day after one of her friends makes her cry her eyes out, she's not better off staying at home where you can shield her from undue pain. You've never had to worry about predators living nearby, or cyber bullying, or the countless other fucked up things out there in the world now to be outright terrified over."

It's not frustration I hear in his voice, it's something else, something like disappointment. And that's perhaps the toughest thing for me to hear right now.

Logan stares down at me and adds gently, "Until now, you've only had other people's kids to guide. Guide, Nicole, not raise. There's a big difference."

"You're a great therapist," he says in a matter-of-fact way that somehow manages to sound both admiring, and flatly final. "But you're *not* a parent. You're crossing a line right now and if you don't back off, we won't be able to come back from this."

He has a point, an excellent one. I know it. But I have one, too.

"Maybe I am overstepping here," I concede. "You're right. I'm not a parent. I don't know how to be a parent. But you're wrong in thinking that I'm trying to stop or influence your parenting. We each have very different roles. For you as a parent, when your child falls, it's your job to hold her for as long as she needs, to kiss her injuries and make her feel better, make her feel loved and happy in the way that only you can. For me as a therapist, when a child falls, it's my job to help her cope, help her discover and reconcile her thoughts and emotions, help her move past that fall…with none of the same amazing things you have at your disposal."

I feel an ache in my heart I've never felt before as I tell him plainly, "We don't get to be their favorite person in the world, the one who can make them feel better with a hug, the one whose love holds more power than we'll ever have."

He's calmer now, almost thoughtful.

"When she fell off her bike when she was first learning to ride, what did you do?" I ask then.

He glares at me, all calmness back off the table. "Not the same thing."

"No, it's not," I agree. "This is a heck of a lot harder, I know. For both of you. Which means it's going to take more strength from both of you. I know you think I'm in the wrong here, and again, maybe I am. But isn't it possible that I'm also right about this?"

His arms cross his chest as another barrier, even as the anger in his eyes begins to thaw.

"I know I'm not Hannah's parent, and I get that you love your daughter more than any other human being on this planet. But you know the rest of us who've grown to know and care about her love her fiercely as well, right?"

I point out his window to his concerned workers on the floor shooting worried glances our way. "That's why they all told me about Hannah's school troubles to begin with. That's why they've each taken turns teaching Hannah their own personal tips and tricks on the wall. We all love that little girl. None of us would *ever* put her in harm's way. You believe that, right?" I ask. "That none of us would do anything that wasn't in her best interest. That *I* wouldn't be standing here trying to convince you to let her go up if I thought in *any way* that it would be more detrimental than beneficial for her? Do you believe I care about her enough to do right by her in this situation?"

He takes another deep breath.

Before he can answer, Hannah pushes the door open and comes in.

"Dad." She meets his gaze dead-on. "I want to go up again. I know you're scared for me, and I'm scared, too. But, I need you to let me try again." Her voice grows stronger with each word. "And if I fall again, I need you to let me try again after that."

My heart is just about bursting at the seams. A few months ago, she'd never have been able to do this. God, she's come such a long way.

Logan clenches the edge of his desk until his knuckles turn white. "Honey, I want to say yes, but you don't know what fear can do to you up there. I do. I've had the scariest things in my life happen to me. I've lost things I can't ever get back. If you got injured up there, I'd never recover. I'd never forgive myself."

Me, too.

"Please, daddy. Just let me try."

I look over at Logan and see he's wrestling with himself.

"There *is* a way we can reduce the fear factor a little for her," I say, hoping I'm doing the right thing.

Hannah looks over at me. "Really? How?"

I can feel Logan's disapproval over me butting in

again, but despite what he thinks, I'm not here to railroad over his feelings, or his role in his daughter's life and choices. So, I turn to him and simply give him as much info as I can to help him make this difficult decision.

"There've been studies showing how climbing blindfolded focuses the mind and body on the climber's sense of touch over the climber's surroundings."

He's looking at me like I'm nuts, but, I forge on. "Relying only on her sense of touch could help Hannah tune into her body while she's climbing, and offer her brain a constant security that would not be there if she could see her environment. The blindfold dramatically reduces fear by focusing the climber on the task at hand and blocking everything else out. It proved remarkably successful for people who had a fear of heights, which is why I believe it can work here."

I look back at Hannah and put aside all the psychological stuff for a moment. "All that said, sweetie, I want you to understand that you have something I've *never* had in my life. You have someone who loves you so much that no matter how high you climb, how far you go, he is right there with you. Your fears are his fears. So, if he doesn't want you to do this yet, just...try to look at it from his perspective."

My eyes are still on Hannah, but my words are being aimed at Logan as well. "I never had a parent—or anyone—love me the way your dad loves you. Trust me when I say that *not* having that connection to a person, that tether when you're up on a mountain by yourself, makes the climb so much lonelier than it has to be. And so much scarier. If I were lucky enough to have a connection like that with any human being, I'd never do anything dangerous or *reckless* to sever it. Because I can guarantee you that I'd spend the rest of my life wishing I never lost it."

Logan stares at me in stunned silence.

"So just...think about it. Both of you," I say. "I'll leave you two alone to discuss this more. It's a family decision. I'll be right outside, ready to help whatever you decide."

"No. Stay, Nicole." Logan exhales heavily. "Please. I'm asking you to stay."

I think that's the first time he's truly asked and not demanded.

Of course, I stay.

22

| LOGAN |

Between that speech Nicole just delivered and hearing my baby girl stand up for herself the way she did, my brain is on overload.

The way Hannah marched in here and spoke her mind, took charge of her life... Hell, that was something.

Admittedly, a part of me hates it a little bit.

Okay, a lot.

But that doesn't diminish how amazingly proud I am of her, of how much stronger and more confident she's become since Nicole started working with her.

And that's just everything.

But having Hannah climb blindfolded? That's just insane.

It was bad enough when Nicole had her climb with one arm tied behind her back the other week. Sure, it was with a Velcro release so she could use her second arm if she wanted, but the very idea of it had made me nervous as hell.

Nicole's explanation had been sound, of course, having Hannah experience this would cause her psyche to rely on different avenues to accomplish tasks and practice re-routing her decision making and other reactions to help better equip her to cope with things.

That time, I'd let her do it, even with my reservations.

But this…I just don't know that I can be on board with it.

"You could go up with her," suggests Nicole softly. "You could shadow her."

The thought had crossed my mind. "But that would be like a safety net, right? Your therapy wouldn't have its full effect?"

"Yes. You going up there would more be for you than for her."

I love that she never pussyfoots around things.

Turning to Hannah, I gaze into her determined little face. "If you do this, you know there's never any shame in stopping and coming back down, right? Facing your fear doesn't have to happen all at once."

I'm not sure if I'm still talking to her anymore or myself. And Nicole. "Sometimes, it takes a lot of steps, a lot of retries after your fear gets the best of you. And sometimes, you even need to fall in a big way first. All that can be scary, I know. So, if you need to come back down, we will all be here for you."

I exhale a long, heavy breath. "And we'll all be here the next time you try. And the next."

Hannah's watery smile makes that unbelievably difficult declaration all worth it.

"I promise, Dad. I'll be smart. I'll come down and try again tomorrow if I need to."

I shake my head. "That's not smarts, that's strength. And baby girl, you are so strong. I believe in you with all my heart. So go on up, squirt. I'll be down here scared shitless, but supporting you the whole time."

She beams and throws her arms around me.

Before I know it, she's facing her mountain and stretching out again, with all of my free staff cheering her on. I make a mental note to give the whole lot of them raises.

Derick slips the blindfold over her eyes.

And then she's up on the wall.

I don't even realize I'm gripping Nicole's hand until I register her nails digging into my skin.

Every new handhold she grabs shaves another few days off my life, and every time she pauses to choose her next move and then *makes it*, I feel my whole fucking heart overfill just a little bit more with unending pride.

I don't think I breathe until she makes it all the way back down without a single misstep.

"I did it! I did it!" she squeals, ripping off the blindfold and pumping her fist in the air before running to hug me. And then Nicole.

Derick comes over to give her a big hi-five. "That was one righteous climb, kiddo. I'm going to add this to your video highlight reel. Wanna come see it? We've been videotaping you all these weeks. I'll cue it up to the big TV monitor. And I'll make you a copy so you can show all your friends how badass you are climbing blindfolded."

Hannah squeals and runs over to go watch the footage.

Nicole finally let's go of my hand and drops her hands to her knees, her breaths coming in slow and deep, the tension in her frame easing a fraction with each exhale.

I stare down at her face—at the mix of fear and joy I'm sure mirrors my own.

"You didn't answer my question earlier," I say, breaking the silence. "Do you see Hannah as just one of your clients?"

She pauses for a moment before answering softly, "No. That's not how I see her."

Well aware that my staff is staring at us, I grab her hand again and lead her back to my office. Before the door is even fully shut, I continue my interrogation with a gruff, "Earlier, you said you love Hannah. Did you mean that?"

She blinks up at me. "Yes. Yes, I did."

Yeah, I believe it. And that's a good thing. So, what the hell is my issue with it?

Clearly, she's wondering that too. "Does

that…upset you?"

I sigh. "Of course not."

She remains silent, waiting for me to unjumble the mess of thoughts in my head.

Not really sure where to begin, I finally ask her, "Do you know that I've never once heard you say you love anyone or anything before? Not that one time I overheard you talk to your folks. And not even when you talk about those sushi rolls you practically moan over when you eat them."

She looks startled. "Well, the reason I don't say it with my parents is because they don't ever say it to me. Truth be told, I can't actually remember them ever saying those words to me."

Seriously? I yank her into my arms. "I'm sorry, baby. I didn't know."

She shrugs it off. "I'm not going to say it's okay or not. They are who they are. They do love me, I'm sure. Just in their own, silent way. But besides them, you're right, I've never said it about anyone else because I don't really love anyone else. Terrible as that sounds. I don't have any other family to speak of, no super close friends who I could honestly say I love."

She blushes then. "As for those sushi rolls, of course I love them. Apparently, very vocally. I didn't realize I sounded like that when I ate them. I'll make a point not to be quite as…err, *graphic* about it."

"Don't. It's hot as hell." I study her. "What else do you love?"

"Um… Dessert? I love dobash cakes almost as much as sushi."

Not exactly the answer I'm looking for. "Do you love it when I suck on your clit? Tongue fuck that wet, perfect little slit of yours?"

Thank god we're alone. Though honestly, the way I'm feeling right now, I could care less who's listening.

Her breathing gets thinner. "Yes."

"Say it."

"I..." She's fire engine red now, but I don't let her off the hook. "I love it when you make me come," she says instead. "All the ways you make me come."

Dammit, that big brain of hers is sexy. I narrow my eyes on her, wanting more. "Do you love making *me* come?"

This time, her breathing stops altogether for a few beats. "Yes," she whispers. Then she adds without prompting, "I love making you come."

Now for the most important one of all. "Do you love me?"

Her eyes widen. "I…"

Her hesitation is gutting me. And it's possible I'm feeling my fucking heart crack right down the middle.

"I'm scared to," she answers finally. "It's different with Hannah. It's not scary for me to love her."

"But it's scary to love me?"

"It's terrifying."

What the…? *"Why?"*

"Really? Are you seriously asking me that? You who won't engage in anything more than a temporary fling with a woman?"

Well, hell. "Sweetheart, you're more than a fling. And you damn well know it."

"You've never said it out loud." Her voice becomes quietly vulnerable. "Why is that? Is it guilt? Or fear?" she asks softly. "Or is it both?"

"It's not what you're thinking." It truly isn't.

She tilts her head. "What do you think I'm thinking?"

"You're thinking that I'm afraid to get into a relationship with a woman because Janine died and that I'm going to feel guilty about loving another woman."

"Are you? Do you?"

"No. I told you, it's…different."

"So, explain it to me. Please."

Immediately, I feel my throat clogging up with the words I've never actually voiced until now, but I push through. "The day Janine died was both the saddest day of my life because I lost my wife, and also the happiest day of my life because my daughter was born—do you have any idea how something like that can screw with a person's head?"

Of course, she does, she's the head specialist. Still, I

try and explain how it was for me. "It came in waves, the bouts of pain followed by happiness, the avalanches of anger followed by guilt. While it kills me to even *think* it now, shortly after the doctor had told me that Janine didn't make it, I'd wondered—for one brief, awful moment—if we hadn't gotten pregnant with Hannah, if Janine would still be with me."

The immense, unforgiveable shame over that makes my eyes slam shut. "For that one second, I allowed my grief to overshadow my love for my own child."

I open my eyes to gaze down at Nicole's tear-filled ones. "And I've spent my entire life since making up for it. I vowed to myself that day that I would make damn sure that Hannah knows without a doubt in her mind that my love for her is absolute. Second to no one and nothing. From that moment on, Hannah became my entire world."

I cup her sweet, beautiful face in my hands. "Then you came along."

23

| LOGAN |

She's holding her breath so I of course dip down to give her my version of a little mouth-to-mouth. I want to be sure her brain has all the oxygen it needs for this next part.

"Before you, it was easy to have no-meaning flings," I say matter-of-factly. "And frankly, it wasn't really much skin off my dick to keep things like that for the past nine years."

I lock my eyes on hers and say with all the certainty I feel, "I noticed you that first day you walked back into our lives, that first day you climbed in here five years ago. There was something different about you; I almost didn't recognize you as the same girl from college. Then I watched you go up that wall and you took my fucking breath away. You *loved* it up there…bad as you were at it back then."

She gives me an annoyed look and I can't help but

chuckle over how sexy that is too. There isn't much I don't find unbelievably cute about this woman.

"I think a part of me knew from even back then that if I was going to love a woman again, that it'd be you. I didn't get full confirmation of that until recently though."

I shake my head, surprised I'm talking this much about my feelings—the woman really is gifted at this therapy stuff. "The idea of loving you…yeah, it was scary, and yeah, it made me feel guilty. But not because of Janine."

She nods in understanding. "Because of the vow you made the day Hannah was born."

"I spent her whole life living *my* whole life this way. I basically didn't know how to live it any differently. Still don't in fact."

Resting my forehead against hers, I admit softly, "I love you so damn much, Nicole. I love how amazing you are with your students, how incredible you are with my kid. And I fucking love when we're together." I press gentle kisses on her cheeks, after brushing away the tears wetting them.

"Logan, I don't want you to feel guilty about putting me second to your daughter. I'd never expect anything more than that."

I smile. No, of course she wouldn't. And that's what makes her perfect. "How about tied for first? That sound okay to you? Sound all psychologically healthy and stuff?"

More nodding. And more silence. Don't think I've ever heard the woman be this quiet before. It's a bit disconcerting.

"Now," I say. "I'm going to ask you again. Do you love me?"

"Yes," she answers quickly. No hesitation this time.

Best feeling ever.

"Tell me the truth, now that you know the whole story, are you going to start harping on me doing some kind of therapy or something to hash out all my buried feelings and stuff?" I ask, completely serious.

"Oh, my goodness, I'm so glad you brought it up first," she replies, just as seriously. "I can pencil you in for next week after my regulars."

I chuckle. Me and my big mouth. "Depends. Are you going to start telling folks—and by that, I mean the whole damn world—that you love me?" I demand in question form. "Your parents included? I don't care if they have hollow tin chests, they're going to damn well know we love each other."

She grins. "Yes, and yes."

"Are you going to make sure Hannah knows how much you love her? Because she needs to hear it. Every day. I know your folks didn't do that, and you're not used to it, but—"

"Yes," she interrupts softly. "And what's more, I'll want to hear you both tell me the same."

Jesus, why the hell was I such an idiot for the past five years?

"OMG, Dad, just kiss her already!" hollers Hannah over the speaker intercom system blasting through the entire gym. The one we use only for fire drills.

I grin my ass off.

"You did that," I tell Nicole, with no small amount of pride and gratitude. "My once shy, quiet little girl is now that crazy bullhorn-wielding bundle of badass over there."

Nicole chuckles and points over to the big wall TV, currently broadcasting a live feed of my office. We both look up at the far climbing wall and see Derick up there with a video camera, waving.

"We're recording through your window," says Hannah, grinning. "So, make it romantic, you guys."

I do my damndest.

After all the clapping dies down, and the camera is no longer rolling, I gaze down at the incredible woman in my arms and tell her simply, "You're moving back to our place tonight."

"And here I thought we'd made progress on the asking instead of demanding thing," she comments, not sounding terribly bent out of shape over it. "We need to address these bossy tendencies of yours. There are some great therapeutic strategies that can—"

I grab her chin and tilt her head back to kiss her again. Not because I don't want to hear her go all full-shrink on me, but because her talking like this really is becoming some kind of inexplicable turn-on.

"You know," she says when she manages to catch her breath. "That tying one hand behind your back thing would also be very helpful in this situation." She smiles shyly up at me. "Same goes for the blindfold…"

Holy hell.

"I do want to support your psychological endeavors," I say magnanimously as I reach over to pull shut my newly-installed office blinds and yank my phone cord out of its wall socket.

"How about we start my therapy right now?"

Epilogue

| LOGAN |

- Four Months Later -

This was a dumb idea.

I should've fucking gone with something more traditional. Rose petals and a candlelit dinner or something.

Instead, I'm down on one knee on the top of a mountain with Nicole, holding the new climbing carabiner I had manufactured recently.

Since the three of us go climbing together outdoors at least twice a month now, I of course hired someone to make the most top-of-the-line carabiners money could buy. By design, most aren't made to withstand the peak force of more than one average adult person falling at the outdoor heights we typically climb. Mine can handle five times the industry standard.

It's a bit overkill, yes, but I'm not taking any chances

with Hannah and Nicole on the mountain.

Maybe it's lame to be proposing with a clunky metal climbing carabiner instead of a ring, but this, I felt had more significance to this amazing life we're about to have together. As not just man and wife, but as a family.

Thankfully, Nicole thinks so too. If her tear-filled yes is any indication.

All that said, I'm not a total imbecile. I of course got her a diamond as well. A big one. Channel set so she can wear it even when she climbs and a flawless grade capable of catching light and showing anyone with working eyes around her that she's damn well taken.

Before I can reach in my pocket to give her said ring, however, she wipes the tears from her eyes and asks, "Can that carabiner hold four people? Or at least two people, and one person who'll soon be eating for two?"

Proposal, engagement ring, and my own name all but forgotten, I shoot up to my feet and stare at her. "You're pregnant?"

It's not that I wasn't expecting it. Hell, I've been trying to get the woman pregnant from the night she moved back to the house.

Before she can answer, I bombard her with more questions—all the 'therapy' she keeps tricking me into really is doing wonders for me in that regard. "Why on earth did you let me bring you up a *mountain* in your condition?! Have you gone to the doctor yet?" I kiss her before she has a chance to even speak, then I drop to my knees and gently kiss her belly. "Do I get to name the baby?"

"My *condition*," she replies, with her hands on her hips, "has no bearing on my ability to climb, and you know it." Her stubborn gaze dares me to defy her.

My mother didn't raise me to be that stupid.

"Yes, to the doctor," she continues. "No, to the naming part."

"I'm going with you to all your appointments from now on," I growl, placing one last gentle kiss on her belly before getting up to demand, "And why can't I name the baby?"

"Because." She smiles softly. "I thought we could have Hannah pick the baby's name."

Hell, that's a winning trump card and she knows it. "Hannah would love that."

Speaking of which.

I pick Nicole up and sit her down on a nearby rock. "Don't move." I run over to my pack then to get my satellite phone.

She stops me from dialing. "Wait a minute. You're not thinking of doing something crazy like call a chopper to come get me, are you?"

Not going to lie, the thought of an air transport for Nicole did cross my mind. Along with a passing pondering on whether there's an existing patent on a giant bubble bioengineered to keep a pregnant mother from any harm.

SASHA BURKE

I decide it wouldn't hurt to make a few calls.

"Logan, I've read the research. I can climb well into the pregnancy. They have special harnesses and everything."

Yes, yes, my legal team made sure I was well-versed in all of that the first time a pregnant patron wanted to climb in one of my gyms.

Doesn't mean I can't worry my ass off over it.

"I won't call a chopper," I promise, before resuming my dialing.

"Hannah?" I grin into the phone. "Yeah, she said yes."

I pull the phone away from my ear so I don't lose an ear drum when she starts squealing. "Also, Nicole just told me you're going to be a big sister."

This time, I almost do lose an ear drum. Smiling, I switch over to my other ear as she talks excitedly about weddings and babies for a bit before she asks me to hand the phone over to Nicole. "Sure thing, honey. Hang on a sec."

"Hey Hannah," says Nicole in that adoring mom voice I've loved hearing develop over the past few months.

The pair are closer than ever and while I'd been a little jealous of how much they'd bonded at first, now, it's just amazing to watch their connection grow as strong as it has.

For the next minute or so, I listen to Nicole attempt

to get a few words in during the markedly one-sided conversation.

That amazing little girl of mine has turned into quite the conversational bulldozer, who can now argue better than Nicole, even.

When Nicole quietly hangs up the phone a short while later, I look at her expectantly.

"She's sending a chopper," she says with all the reluctantly impressed dignity a woman who just lost an argument to a nine-year-old can muster.

I chuckle.

"It'll be here in one hour."

Interesting. I know for a fact that Hannah could've had one over to us in half that time.

Seriously. Best kid ever.

I make a mental note to raise her allowance.

"One whole hour up here all by our lonesome," I say, pulling my beautiful bride-to-be into my arms as I reach into my pocket.

First I slip the diamond ring on her finger.

Then the blindfold I brought over her eyes.

THE END

*If you enjoyed Logan & Nicole's story,
be sure to check out*

BARE ASS IN LOVE

a hot, sexy rom-com full of dirty, swoony, feel-good fun!

| AVAILABLE NOW |

• • •

Turn Page for Book Info and Excerpt

BARE ASS IN LOVE
by Sasha Burke

THE WOMAN'S KILLING ME.

I'm not the kind of man who would normally even *consider* blurring the lines between landlord and tenant or boss and employee, but Summer is a walking temptation. Neurotic and obsessive-as-hell when it comes to work details, but a damn cute-without-knowing-it temptation nevertheless.

She's been a good tenant and an even better worker. Plus, she doesn't simper or throw herself at me like a lot of women who find out my net worth. I've grown...fond of her, oddly enough.

But if she drags my ass out of bed in the middle of the night to talk about work one more time...

THE MAN'S A SAINT.

Not only did Jason hire me for the greatest project I've ever run point on, but he also let me move into an amazing loft in his building as an extravagant job-relocation perk. Sure, he can be a grouch when I accidentally wake him up to go over the project, but he's still a saint nevertheless.

He's been a fantastic boss and a surprisingly protective landlord. But...when did his shoulders get so wide? And why is that growling voice of his making me all weak in the knees lately?

Also, is it still considered morning wood if it happens in the middle of the night...or something more?

BARE ASS IN LOVE
© 2017 Sasha Burke

| E X C E R P T |

It's no secret that Jason is usually the most handsome man in the room, any room, whether he's in a suit or covered with jobsite dust from head to toe.

But Jason dripping wet and *naked*?

I have no words.

All I see before me are miles of tanned, ripped muscles, and an almost dauntingly impressive erection.

No really. It's *huge*.

And just like that, I can't stop my brain from firing off an onslaught of questions. How does he walk around with that thing and not feel like he has an extra sledgehammer weighing down his tool belt? Would my fingers even meet around it? Do his? Was it that hard this morning when I first saw him at the door?

As I continue to stare, it begins to harden and lengthen even *more*. To the point where I'm not just riveted, but also frankly curious from a general contractor's standpoint. Sort of like that time I once had to figure out how to get a grand piano into the tiny ass little window on the thirtieth floor of a commercial high rise.

Putting the question of seemingly impossible male-female anatomical fit on the back burner for the time being, I shift my silent inquisition to the matter of why he's got a hard-on again. That's the second time today. Is 'morning wood' an ongoing thing? Has he been like this every morning without me noticing? And is it some sort of mysterious biological response for my nipples to be tightening this much now that I *am* noticing?

I feel my cheeks pinking, but I can't seem to pull my gaze away. A hum of warm pleasure begins in my core and I feel my whole body waking up as if I've never really been awake before this moment. It's unsettling. But not in a bad way.

Definitely not a bad way.

Seriously, I need to stop looking at it. He's my boss. And my landlord. I need to look away.

*Any*time now.

Every second that ticks by is another second too long, another second I'm gaping at him like I've never seen a human penis before.

Which is ridiculous for a woman my age. Of course I've seen one.

Well, I've seen porn. And also that one guy in person who hadn't been nearly as hung as Jason. Or whatever the term is for a giant cock now standing upright and all but saluting me.

The unexpected penis-sighting that other time had been an accident, too. The real-life penis guy, not the porn.

I watched the porn on purpose to see what I was missing. Clearly though, my porn research had been a wholly inadequate means of measurement.

Because *wow*.

My heart starts to thunder then, and my brain begins cataloging every millisecond of time passing by. The longer he lets me stand here and look my fill, the more I find myself wondering *other* things. Things so far past improper, I can't even think of the right adjective.

Erotic images beyond anything I'd ever imagined before start swamping my senses, and my brain is suddenly under siege with more illicit questions. Would it feel hot to the touch against my lips? My tongue? How would he react if I reached for him right now? Would he be all cool and collected like he usually is or could I actually break him of his renowned control?

Do I *want* him out of control?

I feel my panties growing damp as the answer to that last question heats me from the inside out, rushing my veins like a drug.

www.sashaburke.com

OTHER BOOKS BY SASHA BURKE

SEXY, FEEL-GOOD FUN
Hot and sweet HEAs with lots of schmexy good times

The HARD, FAST, AND FOREVER Series
BARE ASS IN LOVE *(Available Now)*
HARD ASS IN LOVE *(Available Now)*
GRUFF ASS IN LOVE *(Available June 2018)*

. . . . .

STEAMY & SWOONY ALPHAS
These heroes have <u>one</u> weakness they're finally giving in to…

The Off-Limits and HIS Collection
HIS SHY NERDGIRL *(Available Summer 2018)*

. . . . .

*Want release day links, bonus content, and
fan freebies sent to you throughout the year?*

*Sign up for my EMAIL LIST
http://eepurl.com/cYJpUr*

About the Author

www.sashaburke.com

www.facebook.com/sashaburkebooks

Sasha Burke has been reading romances ever since
she discovered her local library would let her borrow whatever
kind of books she wanted…probably far
younger than she should've started.

Possessive and protective alpha heroes have long been Sasha's
biggest weakness. Reading and writing about them, especially
when there's a feisty heroine involved, has resulted in her
staying up many a night over the years.

You'll usually find Sasha out and about spoiling her
many dogs, or trying to perfect the world's greatest
mac & cheese recipe, or hosting outdoor fajita nights
for her friends as often as she can.

To make sure you never miss a release,

Sign up for my Email List:
http://eepurl.com/cYJpUr

Made in the USA
Coppell, TX
18 August 2023